Blazing Blunderbuss

Wyvern Chronicles

Nix Whittaker

Other Books by Nix Whittaker

Wyvern Chronicles
Blazing Blunderbuss
The Mechanicals
The Jade Dragon
Wyvern's trim and other stories
Ruby Beyond Compare
Lady Golden Hand
The White Lady
The Lady Doctor

Kitsune Shapeshifter Series
Zero Foxes Given
For Fox Sake

Other Books
Once Upon a Midnight

Finally, out of the crawl space, Hara twisted her head first right then left. An inaudible crick produced a sigh from her parched throat. Sweat soaked through her clothes. Her calloused hand ached as she rubbed her equally aching back. The pressure made a spot numb. Short-term relief but enough to get her moving. Hara flexed her fingers which had been too long clenched around tools.

Reaching down she groaned as her fingers closed around the tool belt. The engine hummed and hissed as steam moved through pipes. Her Opa would have been proud of the gleaming knobs and the faint whir of gears. Slipping the tool belt over her shoulder, Hara headed for her cabin. She ran a hand on the wood panelling. The mixture of machine and tooled wood reminded her of home.

It was quiet except for the scrape and hiss of the man in the furnace room. Exhaustion weighed on her shoulders.

Reaching her room, she let her shoulder droop and allowed the tool belt to crash to the top of the table. Bunk beds crowded up against one wall. Her bunk mate absent. He was on the night shift and wouldn't be back till morning. Hara wiggled out of her shirt. Stained with grease and oil, she draped it over the single chair in the room. With her eyelids closed over her itchy and tired eyes, she fumbled for the end of the cloth wrapped around her breasts.

Women weren't normally allowed on airships. Certainly not as engineering crew. The boyish disguise was familiar to Hara, though the wrap around her breasts was a recent addition after she had left the prison. An annoying addition. She flicked the cloth to join her shirt before she poured the remains of her canteen into a bowl nestled into the stand.

Hara stripped out of the overalls, rolled around her waist and stood in her underwear as she washed up with the small amount of water and a sponge.

She dreamed of a soak in a bath.

Her Opa had one outside in his shed. Made for his wife, Hara enjoyed the luxury when she was home. With jets of water, the bath was perfect for massaging sore muscles and getting grease out of all her pores. She shook her head. That particular bath came with conditions she wasn't willing to live with. Including making it easy for her father to find her.

Hara jumped when the door slammed against the wall with a loud thud. A large man stepped into the frame of the doorway. Sailor tattoos of naked women adorned his arms. Hara scowled as she whipped a hand over her exposed parts.

"I knew it." Ivan growled with a dirty finger waving at her. As one stoker for the boiler, she was familiar with him. He gave her a suggestive look, which crawled over every exposed piece of flesh. His meaty arm stretched over the doorframe as he pushed into the room. His size swallowed the space in the tiny cabin as he closed the door behind him. He grinned revealing a gold capped tooth.

Hara backed up and reached behind her for her tool belt. Her hand fumbled while she kept her eye on Ivan.

He stalked closer. "Your hips sway too much like a girl's. You even have long hair."

Which didn't really mean anything, as most of the men in the world's navies had long hair. Her own hair lay across her shoulder but was normally trained into a tight queue.

Ivan flexed his hands in anticipation of grabbing her. This wasn't the first time she had been found out as a girl, but never by the sway of her hips.

Hara's hand found her tool belt and she opened a pocket. She grinned when her fingers closed around a familiar round object.

Ivan grinned back at her. "I see you understand the situation, baby."

She raised an eyebrow. "Do you really think I'm going to do the dirty with you? Well, you have to be dreaming, mate, to think that's going to happen in this lifetime." Her eyes travelled over his grotesque body. He snarled and didn't notice the movement of her other hand.

Hara snapped the latch on the device in her hand and flung it at Ivan. A net sprung from inside, tangling around him. He cursed as he struggled to escape the fine web made from the silk of spiders. Red and white lines ran across his tanned and tattooed skin. They marked the path of the thread, which was otherwise invisible to the eye.

Without waiting for him to free himself, Hara picked up one of her tools to swing at his jaw. The wrench glanced off his chin, a chin in need of a sharp razor blade. Her own jaw ached in sympathy. He went down with a loud thud. Rattling some of the things in the small closet.

She hadn't hit him hard enough to kill him, but he might be out for a while. If discovered in this room, people would assume Ivan was the reason she left, which was only partly true. She was ready to move on. Maybe she wasn't ready to go home yet, but she was ready to stop running.

Working with purpose, she packed her things and dressed. Instead of overalls, she wore a set of leather pants and a loose lawn shirt. She left off the band strapping down her breasts. With the sway of her hips, it wasn't worth it to continue to pretend to be a man.

Once dressed, she strapped on her gear and made sure it wouldn't wiggle loose. She pulled a long, slender wooden box out from under her bed. She slung a leather strap attached to the box over a shoulder as she headed out of her room. She kicked Ivan in passing just for the sake of it.

Hara took the quickest way to the bottom deck, which opened to the air. She stood alone at the turned spindle baluster. She wasn't worried that anyone would find her as most people had settled into bed by this stage of night.

The air cool on her skin whipped at her tied back hair. The pitch-black deck made it difficult to navigate, but she could see the twinkle of a settlement in the distance. Hara did not look forward to wandering around in the empty expanse of the Roshian plateau. At least there was hope of some civilisation out there with the faint flicker of lights.

Hara strapped the wooden box to her back by slipping leather straps through the metal loops over her chest. It made it hard to breathe but better than falling to her death. Satisfied the straps would hold her, she pressed the switch at the base of the case. The box snapped open and wings spanned out. Brass and canvas spanned twice her length to each side of her. Without a glance back at the airship, she stepped into the void and let the wind take her.

———————

Gideon blinked as light eased into the wooden box through a tiny crack. He didn't find himself locked into a wooden box very often, so he watched the crack widen with something more than curiosity. With a loud snap, the lid of the box lifted and slumped next to him.

A group of men stared at him as Gideon looked up at them in return. He didn't jump up and try to escape, as success wasn't likely with the bands around his wrists.

Whoever had organised to kidnap him had known well their task. The bands were made of the elements which had first drawn him to this world, and it made things a little sticky when it came to his ability to change into his true form. When he had woken in the box, he had tried to remove them but they were a set that involved using two hands to disengage the lock. Impossible while wearing them.

After hours in the box and an uncounted time unconscious, Gideon doubted he was in his hometown anymore.

A man growled and all the men peering down at Gideon stepped away. Gideon slowly sat up as his hands were tied together and studied the surrounding room. The seedy and rundown tavern room came complete with peeling and faded wallpaper. The sparse and faded furniture languished, unused by the men in the room. The flower pattern on the fabric now looked like a child's finger painting.

His coffin-shaped box was angled towards the door, where a man stood with his arms crossed over his chest. Men filled most of the room. About half a dozen of them glared at Gideon, though he wasn't sure what he had done to deserve the dark looks. The men all wore tall black boots wrapped with leather straps. Fur dominated their clothes. They sure looked warm, and Gideon wished he had some of their fur, as he was dressed for warmer climes.

Gideon flashed his teeth. "Is it possible for one of you to turn up the heat just a tad? My bones are quite brittle at my age." Everyone ignored his comment as Gideon looked around to find the man in charge.

His eyes landed on the man by the door as he asked in a gravelly voice, "Are you Gideon, the mathematician?"

Gideon studied the man. He wasn't used to being referred to as merely a mathematician. Usually there was an epithet in front of it, like "annoying" or "moron". He rather liked "moron mathematician" as it was an alliteration and there was some symmetry of the insult. He had worked at the university in the capital for the last four decades as a professor, and even they did not call him merely a mathematician.

"I'm a mathematician, but I'm not sure I'm the one you want. I know this mathematician who looks just like me. I'm sure he would be happy to help you out, but I'm afraid my plants are going to miss me. I'm sure they're already wilting."

The man shrugged. Older than most of the others in the room, his beard was peppered with grey. His fur hat covered oily hair and sported two shades of fur.

"I am Nikolai. And if you're a mathematician, then you are the one we want. The men who procured you for us wouldn't have made a mistake lightly."

Gideon studied the other men in the room as Nikolai spoke but the last sentence grabbed his attention. Slowly turning his head back to Nikolai. Gideon asked, "Someone procured me for you?"

Nikolai twitched his nose with his thumb as he thought over his answer. "Yes. You're now in Rosha. You're not in the Empire anymore, Professor." Nikolai's strong Roshian accent made it difficult to understand all his words but Gideon got the gist of it. Rosha stood over a day's train ride to the east from his hometown.

Concern fluttered through Gideon before he clicked his tongue in the classic C'est la vie gesture. "Excellent. I needed a holiday anyway. Does anyone have a drink? Preferably one with one of those olives in it. No?" When they didn't answer him, he demonstrated what he meant with a few gestures, but the men continued to stare at him, so he shrugged his shoulders in disappointed defeat.

Something was off and he couldn't quite put his finger on it. It was the mathematician comment. The reason people never just called him a mathematician was because they could never get over what else he was.

Gideon raised an eyebrow as he realised Nikolai might not know he was a dragon.

———————————————

Hara slapped a coin on the tavern counter. "I'd like a name of an airship which will hire a woman."

Hara decided the previous night as she walked the last mile to the town when she finally came to an epiphany: Her boy disguise only hid her fear of own identity and not her gender. Her father used to dress her as a boy to facilitate his cons. It wasn't like she enjoyed dressing as a boy. It wasn't who she was. Unfortunately, that meant she didn't know herself very well.

Hara's attention returned to the present when the tavern owner put his hand over the coin. She slapped her hand over his so he couldn't retreat with the coin underneath until he told her what she wanted to know.

He sniffed. "There are some captains out back who will take on some women."

She flashed the guy a grin and let him take the coin. At the back of the tavern, several men sat around playing a game of cards.

Hara stepped up to the table and waited for them to acknowledge her. Eventually, one man glanced towards her. His gaze stripped her bare as he licked his lips. "How can we help you, sweetheart?"

She wasn't perturbed by his tone. "I'm an engineer. I'm looking for a berth."

One of the other men chuckled. "You can berth with me, honey."

He patted his knee, suggesting she wouldn't be working as an engineer at all. She sighed. It didn't look like she would find a berth any time soon. She flashed her teeth as she went for one of her gadgets.

———————————————

Nikolai left with many of the men. A few guards remained behind with Gideon to make sure his clothes were appropriate for the climate. Gideon stalled by insisting he needed food.

"I feel a bit faint." Placing a hand to his forehead in dramatic fashion. They ordered a meal of borsht for him. He enjoyed playing the role of the academic fop but once the meal was over, the men tied his hands in front of him again. Leaving the bands on.

As they pushed him out of the room, Gideon raised his arms up. "Is there any way we can make these just a tad more comfortable? I'm afraid I have very delicate skin, which is getting all scratched up by this very, very coarse rope. You don't happen to have silk, do you?"

The men shoved him forward. Gideon ignored their roughness and carried on trying to distract them.

"Mmm, silk," he said nostalgically. "Well, I suppose you two aren't that adventurous. But trust me, silk rope is an excellent investment. It doesn't chaff."

The two guards shoved Gideon again to make him move, but Gideon stopped. "I rather like silk rope. You'll be surprised at what you can do with it. But this rope is so scratchy. Well, if you don't have silk, then can you take off these bracelets? They pinch against the rope. See?" He shoved his wrists into the face of the guard as they maneuvered him out of the tavern and onto the street.

"They're all pink, and aren't they just ghastly? Way too girly for me. I mean, I like my clothes pink and such, but that doesn't mean I don't like women. Remember the silk ropes." He wiggled his eyebrows suggestively but the two guards were not interested. "I suppose pink bracelets is a little kinky but I was never into it. Ropes can be fun but pain was never my thing."

Gideon sighed as the guards were oblivious to his suggestion. It would seem he would have to find another way to achieve his freedom.

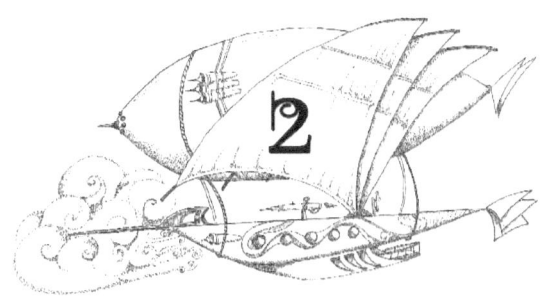

Shoved out of the tavern, Hara swore at the men and ducked when they threw her glider at her. It clattered on the cobblestones of the alleyway. Hara picked it up to see if they had damaged it. Left alone in the empty alley, the door to the tavern shut. Satisfied she had convinced them that no matter their desire for her, she would be more trouble than pleasure.

Hara ran her hands over the wooden sides of the glider case. Placated, it was still in good shape except for the scratches on the side. A door opened further down the alleyway and two men shoved another man out. With his hands tied in front of him, he stumbled and regained his balance.

The imprisoned man turned to the others. "Hey, I'm delicate here. There's no need to be so shovey and pushy. Remember, I'm just a professor. I don't have a weapon. I'm not going to hurt you, so you don't have to be so—so violent. And with all this movement, I really don't want to see my dinner again. No matter how lovely it was."

He attempted to smooth his hair away from his face, but with his hands tied together, it was an awkward action. Dressed in an oversized fur coat with a tweed jacket showing underneath, he certainly didn't fit in with the Roshian commoners who held him captive. The Roshians, armed to the teeth—though being armed was not surprising in a smugglers' port, exuded menace.

Hara hesitated. She hated fops. Less than useless, she thought. She needed to find a way out of the town and find a permanent berth. She didn't need to get into fights with random Roshians. Sighing, because she knew it really didn't matter. Hara couldn't leave a person in trouble. Trouble and her were close enough that she wondered some days whether it was hereditary to seek him out.

Hara called out, "Hey, I don't think the toff wants to go with you guys!"

All of them turned. The prisoner motioned with his tied hands to shoo her away. "That is awfully sweet of you to say that, but these guys aren't about to play nice. I wouldn't want you to get hurt or anything. As long as they remember I'm delicate, I'll be fine. Especially if they remember to use silk rope next time." He grinned as if it was merely a game of sorts and he wasn't being kept prisoner.

At least he was a decent guy. That made it almost a good idea to help him. Almost. She approached, dropping her glider to the ground to help with her agility.

One of the Roshian men said, "Get lost, *malenkaya devotshka*. This is not your problem."

Hara replied in Rosh, "I'm afraid I have the bad habit of making things my problem."

One of the Roshian men held the prisoner so he wouldn't escape and the other pulled out a large Barker Iron. There were more sophisticated weapons on the market, but it was big enough to put a pretty large hole in her. The Barkers were a favourite of Roshian revolutionaries, to the point that the revolutionaries were called Rosh Barkers after their weapon of choice.

Hara took another step closer. "If you let him go, no one has to be hurt."

The two Roshian men looked at each other in confusion. The one with the gun turned to her. "You do realise there are two of us and only one of you?"

Hara grinned with her hands spread out to appear harmless. "I know. It doesn't seem fair, does it? Maybe if I tie one of my hands behind my back, it might even the odds."

She took another step forward and the men who remained still. Maybe going around as a girl without a disguise was a good idea. If she had been dressed as a boy, she would have been attacked already.

Hara waved her hands as she spoke. "I mean, you can't even call for help. This alleyway is completely deserted. I doubt the people in the tavern will even rouse if they hear a minor scuffle out here."

She used the waving of her hands to disguise her movement and took the final step she needed to get close enough to the gun-waving Roshian.

Hara moved fast. Setting her feet apart for stability, she knocked his gun aside and stepped into his guard. She pulled her arm back and slammed the ball of her palm into the man's throat. He doubled over and she helped him over a little further into her knee. He grunted and slumped to the ground, unconscious.

The other Roshian fumbled for his gun, but his prisoner saw the opportunity for escape and struggled against his hold. Hara grabbed the Roshian's gun. She slammed the metal handle into the man's face and knocked him out.

Now that she had dealt with the Roshians she turned back down the alley to picked up her glider, still in its box.

The fop followed her. "Thank you. The rescue I mean." He waved with his tied hands to indicate the alleyway and the downed men.

Hara shrugged. "You don't happen to have a spare airship available?"

He shook his head. "I'm looking for one myself, though. We can look for one together."

Hara picked up her pace. "That's nice for you. But I think it might be better if we are on our own."

She certainly would be better off without a fop following her around.

She headed out of the alley and down the street. The fop followed. He worked the knots out of his restraints with his teeth as he skipped to keep up with her.

Hara considered the airships floating above the town. She might not get a job on one of them, but she knew enough about airships to stow away. And she needed to get out of town before the men she had knocked out woke and informed the others. Only an idiot would make enemies of the Rosh Barkers and stick around to see what they would do about it.

Hara picked up her pace, but the fop managed to keep up with her. She bet he would still keep up with her, even if she sprinted. Stopping at the wooden palisades which marked out the boundary around the port, large rocks with metal pins lined up in a row indicated the anchors for the airships. Men milled around. Some lounged on stools at the base of their ships or on the decks of their ships. Large wooden crates piled up around the edge of the port, ready to be loaded by steam-powered lifts. Porters lugged crates to them, which then rose sluggishly to the awaiting airships.

Hara moved behind the crates and crouched. Peeking over the top, she analysed the different ships. Five ships floated above the large field. A sleek runner drifted near them. It wouldn't have a large cargo hold, but it would be fast. It was an armed ship with large guns mounted on the sides which loomed to cast a shadow over the crates she hid behind.

Most likely a pirate rather than a smuggler. A little more dangerous, even for this town. The sleeping guard leaned back in his chair, but she dismissed the ship as too much trouble. If discovered on it, she would be killed rather than dumped overboard at a low altitude or over water. Though a beautiful ship, she'd pick another ride to avoid trouble.

The fop flopped next to her. "You're very agile. I could hardly keep up with you. I like that."

Hara glared at him. "That was the point. I told you I thought we should split up."

The fop, oblivious to the bite in her tone, popped his head up over the crates. Then ducked back down just as quickly.

He asked, "Which one are you going for?"

Hara peered over the top of the crates again. The distracted guard lounged by a large-bellied hopper. Made for brief trips with a large cargo area, good for smuggling along the border. The guard flirted with a girl, enticing her to spend some time with him. It would be a simple task to sneak past him and climb the ladder hanging from the deck of the ship.

Hara prepared to move for the hopper when a commotion at the gate of the port made her glance that way. Several Rosh Barkers pushed their way past people. She swore and ducked down again.

She turned to the fop. "You just made things very difficult."

He glanced over the top. "Mmm, those men again. I'm afraid they chased all the girls away as well."

Hara hoped he wasn't right when she looked over the crates again. The sweet-talking guard pulled out his gun while the girl disappeared. She swore.

"The guy over there is still asleep," said the fop, as he gazed over at the sleek runner. "He sure does have a pretty ship. Almost as pretty as you are." He flashed her a grin but didn't expect anything from his flirting, as he was already looking at the ship again.

The sleek runner would be a possibility, except the Rosh Barkers would see them going for it before they could complete the climb. They wouldn't be able to hide away until the ship left on its own, like she had wanted to do before. Besides, the runner was still a pirate, and the crew wouldn't be very forgiving.

Hara ducked to hide again, intending to make a new plan when the fop moved. He went for the sleek runner. Crouched low, he dashed across the empty space between the crates and the anchor the ship was tied to. The guard didn't even stir as the fop started climbing the rope.

The Rosh Barkers noticed him though and yelled as they spotted him, and she swore. That fop was going to get her killed. She shouldn't have rescued him. He was trouble when she first saw him. Well, she thought, in for a penny, in for a pound.

Hara ran and threw a few flash bangs into the crowd. Yelling and smoke engulfed the port as it exploded. Gun shots echoed off the crates, but with the smoke, they were shooting blind. She went by memory into the smoke. She squeezed her eyes shut and wished she had the time to put on her goggles.

Hara felt for the rope and cut it with a knife once her fingers found a firm grip. She was yanked off her feet by the buoyancy of the runner. Swinging, she climbed the rope. The fop was more agile than she could have imagined, as he was already pulling himself onto the runner and over the railing.

With still a chance that there were people on board, she was cautious. It was rare for a ship to be left in port without even a single sentry, even if they had someone set up on the ground. The fop had no weapon and no chance against a pirate sentry.

Hara climbed faster. At the top, she pulled herself on board. She wrangled herself over the railing.

She jolted when someone flew past her. The man thunked on the ground below. He groaned and moved, so they weren't high enough to kill anyone by throwing them overboard.

The fop dusted off his hands as she finished climbing aboard. She yelled, "You could have killed him!"

The fop glanced over the edge. "He lived? Oh, what a pity."

She shook her head. The man was crazy. Maybe she should have left him with the Rosh Barkers. She heard a commotion further in the airship. Another crewman had discovered the fop.

The crewman said, "Hey, what are you guys…" He stepped back when she pulled a gun on him. Unarmed, he quickly surrendered. He put his hands up. "Hey, no need to get all violent here. If you want to take the ship, I'm up for it."

Hara looked the man over. Covered in soot and grease, he was probably the man who stoked the boiler. Scrawny, he had a bruise half-hidden by the soot on his cheek. She narrowed her eyes as she took in his appearance. This man wasn't a pirate.

The fop came forward and patted the man on the shoulder. "Perfect. We'll need a crew."

Hara glared at the fop. How did he think they would work a ship that usually had a dozen men to fly it?

The man looked at her and the fop. "So, who's in charge?"

The fop said, "Don't look at me. She is. I don't do leading. Too much responsibility for me." He wriggled his fingers to indicate he didn't want to get his hands messy.

Hara rolled her eyes. The fop passed by the crewman and wandered further into the ship. The crewman watched him go, then looked at her. She put her gun away and the man didn't seem inclined to fight.

Hara asked, with a nod to the bruise on his cheek, "Did they treat you alright?"

The man shrugged. "As good as can be expected. They could have killed me when they took my ship, but they kept me because they were short of a few men and needed someone to stoke the fires."

She had heard this story before and it told her what she had suspected—that this was a pirate ship.

She said, "I'm Hara. What is the name of this ship?"

"The Blazing Blunderbuss," the man answered.

She shook her head at the ridiculous name of the ship. It could be worse; at least the name didn't denigrate women.

The crewman followed her as she went further into the ship.

He asked, "What do you intend to do, Captain?"

Hara glanced at the man. "What's your name?"

"I'm Henry, sir. I used to be a cook on an empire cargo ship."

Hara moved rapidly through the ship. "Well, Henry, I don't really have any plans. But that crazy fop seems to attract trouble, so I hope we don't end up dead after all this."

Henry looked to where the fop had disappeared and asked, "Who is he?"

Hara shrugged. "No idea, but I think I should find out." She made it to the bridge and turned to Henry. "Stoke up the boilers. I think we might need some power, and very soon."

Henry disappeared and she turned to the fop, who stared out the window of the bridge. Completely oblivious to the fact he had just stolen a pirate ship. The bridge was decorated with turned wood. Gold leaf was still evident on some decorations, though most had faded.

Hara yelled, "What the blazes were you thinking? This is a pirate ship. We'll have more than the Roshians on our tails after this."

He turned to look at her. "I suppose so, but I thought the ship was just going to waste. Ain't she a beauty? The crew obviously didn't appreciate her. Just leaving her there with hardly any crew at all." He smoothed a hand over the nicked and dirty wood frame around the window.

"Her name is the Blazing Blunderbuss," Hara stated.

He grinned, flashing white teeth. "What an awful name. See, I was right. They don't appreciate her. You'll be a much better captain. Maybe give her a better name. Though I do like that, it's an alliteration."

What delusions must he have floating in his head to think that she wanted to be captain of a pirate ship?

"But I'm not a captain," she said. Even as she said this, she could feel an echo inside that whispered that this could be home. A home her father would never find.

He blinked gold eyes at her as he asked incredulously, "Why not?"

Hara threw her hands up in the air in exasperation. Why was she arguing with a madman, anyway? She ignored him and went to the wheel. With a glance at the charts, she set the wheel and turned back to the fop.

He stared at her. "See, you are perfect!"

Hara glanced back at the charts, exasperated. "Only a moron wouldn't be able to read charts."

He came up to her side. "That's true, but these are all in code. A lovely code. Look, it doesn't even use letters." He traced his fingers over the papers.

She snorted. "A common code, and though lovely, it's simple. It has to be. Pirates aren't the brightest of

20

cookies. Anyone who has spent even a modicum of time on an airship will be able to read these."

He looked over the charts again and glanced at the window, ignoring her argument. "So where are we going, Captain?" he asked instead.

Hara growled. "I'm not a captain. I'm Hara, I'm just an engineer."

He flashed her a grin. "A cute engineer."

She huffed. Her eyes went to the heavens and asked the gods for patience. "This is not the time to flirt. We could have pirates on our tails and Rosh Barkers wanting to kidnap you again."

His eyes sparked. "You think I'm flirting with you?"

Hara narrowed her eyes. "This is not the time."

He said with a lopsided smile, "Gideon. My name is Gideon. Is Hara your full name, or is it a nickname? Harrrra, Harrrra." He rolled the "r" and played with it on his tongue.

She had had enough of this. She stalked up to him. "I didn't save you because I thought you were cute or because I liked you."

He didn't seem intimidated at all by her tone or proximity. He stared at her with his gold eyes. "Then why did you save me?"

Hara sighed. "Because, apparently, I'm a sucker. Now go find something useful to do. I have to get us out of here before the original owners of the Blazing Blunderbuss track down another ship to come after us."

Gideon shrugged at her suggestion. "Are you going to tell me where we're going?"

She answered in a defeated tone. "Home. I'm going home." And apparently she was taking a madman with her.

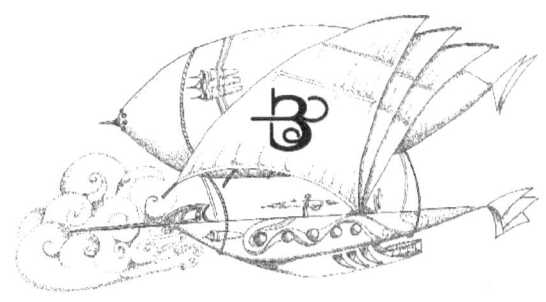

Gideon looked over the terrain. He had been here many years ago when he had first come to this planet. It was so lush and green compared to the fireball he had left behind.

All the dragons on planet Earth were refugees. They had left their own planet because it had come too close to a comet and was mostly a wasteland of fire. When it was deemed that their world was dying, all their scientists had gotten together. They had come up with two plans.

One was to dig into the crust of the planet and live underground. Since they were a race of flyers, many had deemed that a fate worse than death. The females embraced this plan more than the males, as they were used to laying eggs in caves and feeling the earth all around them.

The other plan was for them to abandon the planet altogether and leave for another plane. They had some success going to places which were like their own by using elements which were common to both realms. After the comet had destroyed their planet, the scientists had scrambled for these elements. In the end, they had used petrified wood and the horn of an animal along with a stone that grew from crystals. They had brought the dragons here.

Most of the dragons who had come to Earth had been male, as the females had stayed behind with a few males who could breed with them. When Gideon had arrived here, he had thought he gave up his chance for family and adding a female to his collection. Most of the other dragons had been bitter and had attacked the humans. If they could not procreate, then they could at least collect.

Gideon had come for the sky.

He turned to look at Hara. She worked with the log books left by the previous owners. Maybe he could do some collecting of his own, after all. He had heard of the others bonding with humans, and it allowed them to fully come to this plane. That meant breeding with a human woman and having children; a dream many of his kind had abandoned when they had come here many years ago.

Some dragons had bred with human women, and many of the children still could change into a dragon, though humans had no inkling of the half-breeds' ability. These children were mostly nobility. Gideon had never bothered with politics. Dragon or human.

Gideon hadn't realised he desired a family until he had seen Hara stepping into trouble to save a stranger like him. Now all he had to do was convince her that she wanted to be part of his collection.

———————————

Gideon was pressed up against the glass of the bridge like a child against a candy store window. He said almost conversationally, "Hara, I think you might want to see this."

Hara had read through the logs to see exactly whom they had taken the airship from. The ship only went to ports which were in the no man's land between the Empire and the rest of the world, so they were definitely pirates or arms smugglers. They were not people anyone wanted to mess with.

Hara was not amused to be interrupted. "What?" She snapped the word out and glanced up. Her hands went limp and she dropped the log book.

Another airship approached them at speed. Hara swore and rushed to the window. There were no flags on the airship, but the envelope that held its helium was painted black. It must be the pirates coming for their ship. Except it came from the wrong direction. There were mountains close by though—probably where the pirates lay in wait for someone to come close enough for them to attack.

Darn it, they had fallen into a trap and it was plain bad luck. She glared at the fop. He had brought bad luck right from the start. With a crew, she would have probably tried to run or fight back. With only the three of them on board, they didn't have any real options, except maybe to die horribly or die quickly. Hara decided she would die fighting.

Hara rushed to the speaking tube. She yelled, "Henry, we have company. Stoke it up."

Henry's voice replied over the tube. "Aye aye, Captain."

Hara spun the wheel and said to Gideon, who was still staring out the window, "Maybe you could be useful and man one of the guns. Otherwise, it won't matter how fast we are. Not that it'll matter, we're dead meat, anyway." The last bit, she muttered to herself.

Gideon turned to her. "You don't think you can outrun them?"

She worked vigorously at half a dozen crewmen's jobs on the bridge. "Not today. We would need more crew to man the boilers to be able to outrun that, let alone trim sails so we can manoeuvre. I'd be tempted to shoot them out of the sky, but we don't even have enough crew to man all the guns."

He came up to her and offered his hands. "Take these off."

Hara heard the crack of a cannon blast and spun the wheel to avoid it. The Blazing Blunderbuss shuddered as the cannon ball clipped one side of the ship.

Gideon shoved his wrists in her face and demanded, "Take these off now!"

Hara shoved him away. "I don't think we have time for this, Gideon. We're about to be killed by a bunch of thieving pirates."

He caught her arm. "We will be if you don't remove these bands right now."

She looked down at his wrists and saw he was wearing ivory and ebony bracelets with some sort of pink quartzn inlaid. A little girly, but then, he was a fop. They were tight, so they weren't the kind that were slipped over the hands. Instead, there was a lock on one side and hinges on the other. The lock was a simple thing, but it needed two hands to unlock it.

Hara grabbed his wrists and snapped off the first bracelet. She did the same to the other and turned back to the wheel. She said over her shoulder, "Now go put some holes in those pirates."

He disappeared without a comment. She stared at his retreating back. They were definitely going to die if they couldn't even shoot back. A series of cracks and the airship shuddered and creaked as wood shattered. The engine wheezed and she knew it wouldn't be long before they were in serious trouble.

An air current hit the side of their airship, buffeting them. She struggled to keep her footing and to keep the ship on course as the whole craft tilted sideways. The window on the bridge darkened as something flew in front of it. All she saw was gold scales. Heck, it was a dragon.

Hara tried to get the airship to move, but the wheel was unresponsive. That last hit must have been to the rudder or to one stabiliser on the side. With the dragon in the air as well as the pirate, they really had no chance. Hara closed her eyes for a moment and prayed to the gods to take her soul out of the hellfire she was in.

She braced for the dragon to attack, but it didn't attack their ship at all. Instead, it turned on the other ship. She went to the window to look out at the pirate ship and the golden dragon.

The dragon wrapped itself around the wooden ship and ripped into the envelope above it like a two-year-old at a birthday party opening presents. The pirate ship lost altitude quickly.

The dragon flapped his large leathery wings and pulled away. The pirate airship sank down, and it was clear it would not be a problem any longer. The dragon hovered for a moment, then headed towards them.

Hara ran back to the wheel. She wasn't sure what she could do against a dragon, but she wasn't going to go down without a fight. The airship shuddered, but nothing else happened.

She turned when Gideon walked in. He tucked his hands into his pockets and walked to the windows to look outside again.

Hara asked, "Where the heck did you go?"

Gideon glanced over his shoulder and had to flick his head to get his hair out of his eyes long enough to actually look at her. "I thought I'd go for a walk."

He turned back to look out of the window.

She opened her mouth to demand an explanation when things clicked in her head. She set the wheel and stalked up to him.

Hara asked, her voice a little shrill, "Are you a dragon?" He turned to face her fully and leaned against the frame of the window. His eyes were warm as he gazed at her.

Gideon asked, "Is that going to be a problem?"

Hara blinked in confusion at his nonchalant tone. "A problem? You're a dragon!" her words went high pitched near the end of her sentence. She coughed to cover her embarrassment at sounding like a harpy.

Obviously concerned about her answer. "Yes. But I asked you if it'll be a problem. I kind of want to know your answer."

He was a dragon. The kind that ate people. Why would he care what people thought of him, let alone her? She studied him for a long moment, waiting for her thoughts to unscramble, until she could string some words together. "Why the heck would it be a problem that you're a blasted dragon? You're a dragon, you can do what the heck you like. You can leave right now if you want to. Go anywhere you like."

That meant he hadn't really needed rescuing in the first place. When he had assured her he would be fine, he had been telling the truth. She had followed him onto this darn ship because she had been worried about him, but he hadn't needed the ship either. Her anger was supplanted for a moment by confusion.

"Why didn't you just fly away when we were in the smuggler's port?" Hara frowned as she asked the question. Maybe it was better to change the subject anyway, as she wasn't comfortable with her own anger.

He motioned to the ivory bracelets, which were lying on the wooden boards by the wheel. "They stopped me. That's why I got you to take them off. I think we should put them away, don't you?"

Gideon stepped past her and collected up the bracelets. Hara followed him, stunned by his revelation.

"What's a dragon doing here?" she asked. "I mean in a smugglers' port. You were being kept prisoner by a couple of Rosh Barkers."

Gideon tucked the bracelets away in one of his pockets and nodded, as if that answered the question. He was so frustrating. He was looking out the window to the side. Probably checking out the damage the ship had taken.

The engine still whined. She went to the tube and called down. "Henry, let the engines idle. We don't need the power and I don't want to blow it."

"Aye, aye, Captain," Henry replied automatically.

Hara turned back to the dragon.

Gideon said, "It might be difficult to get anywhere with the damage. I'm sorry it took me so long, but I needed to get some distance away from the bands."

Hara shook her head. He was a dragon. She could hardly get her head around the fact that there was a dragon in front of her. Dragons had once eaten humans and burned them to crisps. But a few hundred years ago, they made a treaty with humans. Now the nobility were mostly half-dragon, half-human hybrids.

The dragons could have taken over the government if they had wanted to, but they did not crave power in the same way that humans did. They usually collected things. Money, treasure, and even humans. Slavery was outlawed, but dragons did not consider the humans in their collections to be slaves. They also never took things from people who looked after them.

Hara thought that was the main reason they hadn't seized power from humans. They must have approved of whatever the governments were doing to look after their people and lands.

Hara worried one day that attitude might change if humans ever took advantage of the people under their care.

No one had ever explained to her why it was different if you were owned by a dragon, because she had never met a dragon before and would probably have gone her whole life without meeting one if she hadn't stumbled upon Gideon. Most commoners never met a dragon in their lifetime. She had hoped to be so blessed. Unfortunately, she had never been very lucky, and recently luck had not been her friend.

Hara said, "So what's stopping you from flying away now?"

Gideon glanced at her as if amazed by the suggestion. He looked over his shoulder out to the side stabilisers. "I think I'll stick around a little longer. You might need me."

She went to the window to assess the damage. The stabiliser was there, but it was flapping in the wind. If they didn't secure it soon, it would snap off and they would have to replace the whole thing. Hara asked, "Can you make sure we don't lose bits of the ship?"

Gideon grinned at her. "I knew you wouldn't mind that I was a dragon."

Hara wrinkled her nose. "You're useful. We'll discuss your being a dragon later."

She turned when Henry came onto the bridge.

"Man, that was close."

Hara had to agree with him. "And bad luck. We're badly damaged."

Henry asked, "The place we're going to, does it have the facilities to fix this kind of damage?"

Hara looked out the window again at the stabilisers. "My Opa is an engineer. He'll fix this in a jiffy. If I had the tools, I could have fixed it myself. His place isn't very far from here; it was where we were headed, anyway. It's more than time I visited my hometown. After that, you two can go anywhere you like. Preferably back to your homes."

Henry ran a hand through his hair. "That might be difficult for me. You see, the Empire—and well, most countries don't look so kindly on people who work on pirate ships."

Hara frowned at him. "But you were taken. You're a victim. Surely they can't blame you."

Gideon spoke up. "They'll say he should have died."

Hara snorted. There were always options when you were alive. But she saw the point. Regardless of whether or not Henry had been forced, he would be considered guilty.

Gideon stepped closer to her. "I also don't really want to go back home. You see, I was minding my own business when some people kidnapped me. I think floating around all over the place will make me just a tad more difficult to kidnap."

She turned to glare at him. She was going to say he was a dragon and could look after himself perfectly well, but she noticed Henry was listening intently. It might be better to keep Gideon's identity a secret for the time being.

She flapped a hand at him and he just flashed her a grin. She said firmly, Like you would to a puppy when training him, "You might be safer at home."

His grin only grew broader.

The insufferable lout. But he had saved her life, so she would tolerate him for a little longer. She would need all her attention focused on their destination, anyway.

Hara hadn't been home in years. Her father had destroyed her faith in family. She had walked away from him and his schemes. At first she had intended to go back, but she knew that her Opa's home was no longer her own. So she had taken the long way home, and that had been two years ago.

She wasn't looking forward to this homecoming.

———————

Gideon held onto the side of the Blazing Blunderbuss. The ship tipped with his extra mass as he made sure the stabilising sails on the side of the ship weren't going anywhere.

He let go of the airship and dropped back, snapping his wings open at the last moment. Spinning in the air he grazed the ground with a claw before he moved his wings and pulled himself up. He flew a few laps around the airship before bringing himself to the deck. Before changing back into his human form.

Henry came past and he looked up from some food stores in his hands. He frowned. "What are you doing out here?"

Gideon grinned. "Just getting some air."

Henry nodded and turned his attention back to the food. "I hope you like coq au vin. Man, I miss cooking."

Henry was gone before Gideon could give an answer either way. He seemed like an easy-going fellow and Gideon wondered if Hara realised she had already added the man to her collection.

Gideon sauntered on to the bridge. Hara had her head bowed as she worked on something. Brass pieces and a tool box at her side. He watched her for a long moment. Her hands were delicate and moved like a witch casting an incantation. He asked, "What are you making?"

Hara didn't look up as she answered. "I'm putting in a mount so I can put a chair up here for you to sit on. At the very least, it should give you something to hold on to if we ever have to move suddenly." She looked up at him and asked, "You secure the sails?"

He nodded. "They'll be fine until we can get into a port."

Hara thanked him and went back to her work. She didn't notice when he continued to watch her. It was kind of her to put in the chair for him.

After a while, he went to explore the rest of the ship. There were a few small rooms and a large stateroom. He was tempted to move into it and see what Hara did about it, but he knew he would have to work slowly with her. She reminded him of a deer. A little skittish.

He finally settled himself in one of the cleanest rooms and lay down to sleep. He felt comfortable on the ship, a bit like how he felt when he was working on a theorem with other mathematicians. That moment when everything clicked together and the part he had played in it all—amazing—he could feel that without having to do anything. He fell asleep with a smile on his lips.

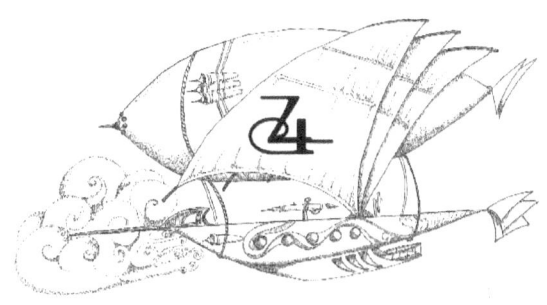

The Blazing Blunderbuss limped into the outskirts of the small town near sunset. Hara yelled for Gideon to drop anchor well outside the town centre. There was no one to set the anchor, so they let it drag on the ground until it dug in. The whole ship jerked and shuddered before it settled.

Henry called up from the engine room. "She's all put to bed, Captain."

Hara had instructed Henry to idle the engines down, and for the last few miles they had been cruising on the leftover momentum and the wind. They could have arrived earlier, but they would have risked more damage to the engine and the airship.

Gideon came to stand next to her. "It looks quaint."

Hara would have said "sleepy" if she had been in a good mood, or likened it to a one-horse town where the horse had died and been buried. There were no other airships, but there were plenty of steam engines in the courtyard outside her Opa's workshop.

Opa took in all the vehicles in the area for repairs and he often invented his own as well. His workshop was the largest building in the small town. There were some stores and a few houses, but most people lived further out on their farms.

Hara kicked the ladder over the edge and it clattered and almost reached the ground.

Henry sidled up next to her and Gideon. "You alright with me wandering around for a bit? I haven't been off the lady in almost a year."

Hara said, "It's your choice. You aren't a prisoner anymore. We'll be around for a day or two while we do repairs. We'll be at that workshop over there." She pointed to her Opa's workshop and then started down the ladder. The others followed behind her.

She wasn't worried about setting a guard as there wasn't anywhere the ship could limp off to in its current condition. All the gear on board was locked up and she had the keys. The pirates had kindly left them in the stateroom.

Gideon was down next. He looked around at the town and tucked himself into Hara's shadow. Once Henry was down, he scuttled off and Hara wondered if they would ever see him again. It would be difficult to get the airship moving without someone in the engine room. Hara doubted she could convince Gideon to shovel coal.

Anna came out of the post shop situated on the edge of the landing field. She was there late, but that wasn't unusual. She leaned against the door of the shop. "Haven't seen you in a while. I thought you died or something."

Hara ignored the tone. Anna was always grumpy. Anna pushed away from the door and came over to give her a hug. A little tighter than usual, which meant Anna had probably worried about her. Hara felt guilty. She should have at least sent a letter to tell them she was fine. Even better than fine. She had finally escaped her father.

Anna said softly against Hara's hair, "Too long, my girl. Too long." Anna looked over her shoulder to Gideon and asked, "So, is this your man? He's yummy." She wiggled her eyebrows suggestively.

Hara rolled her eyes. "Anna, I'm not going to settle and start having babies. This is—" Hara stalled. She still didn't want to tell people Gideon was a dragon. She wasn't sure what he was to her, either.

Gideon stepped forward and offered his hand. He grinned at Anna. "Are you family to Hara?"

Anna looked him up and down without any shame. "You could say that. Her mother was never in the picture and Alfred has never been good with kids. Look at the mess he made with her father. Reckless cad he is." She patted Hara on the cheek and turned to Gideon. "You look after her and make lots of babies."

Hara sighed. She wouldn't be able to change Anna's mind now. Hara walked towards the workshop without caring if Gideon followed her or not. Anna would look after him if he went for a wander.

⸺⸺⸺⸺⸺⸺

Anna went back into the post shop and Gideon followed. He tucked his hands in his pockets so he wasn't tempted to fiddle with the things in her place. He often forgot that certain things weren't his and tucked objects in his pocket as easily as he tucked his hands away. That particular habit had gotten him into a lot of trouble over the years, and not just with humans.

Gideon asked, "What was she like as a child?"

Anna chuckled. "You got it bad, don't you, boy?" She didn't seem surprised he had followed her or that he was asking questions.

Gideon said, "I want her to be part of my collection. I'm not having much luck convincing her about the merits of that though. I was hoping you could give me a few tidbits I could use."

Anna leaned against the table she sorted the mail on and studied him for a long moment. Eventually she asked, "Dragon?"

He nodded. "I'm a little confused that people don't recognise me. I mean, I've lived amongst humans for a very long time and I've never been mistaken as human, and yet there have been a few recently who haven't recognised my nature."

Anna said, "We don't get to see many dragons out here. Maybe the people you're used to dealing with are people who are always around dragons. Most people still think of dragons as either a distant menace or as nobility. Both are to be feared and catered to."

Gideon thought about her words as he wandered the room and looked at the postcards pinned to the wall. They were from places all around the world. He asked, motioning to the postcards, "Are these to you?"

Anna said, "Some, but most of them are for Alfred."

Gideon nodded taking in this new information. He recognised the name on the cards. "He was very popular in his day. The other nobles didn't understand why he would give it all up for his wife. The other dragons, they understood."

Anna smiled warmly at the thought of the woman. "She was certainly an awesome woman, but she didn't like the crowds."

Gideon remembered the plump woman with fire in her eyes. "Agoraphobic. She was still brilliant, though. I always wondered what they would do together," he said distractedly as he looked around.

Anna flashed a knowing grin. "They've made some things, but I don't think the world is ready for them."

The dragon had to agree. Alfred, in his day, had been inventing weapons. Mildred, Alfred's wife, had also been an inventor, but she had been making crystals which could make machines do things by rote. Anything they made would be devastating. He didn't doubt for a minute they had made something spectacular, and he was glad they had never unleashed it on the world.

Gideon asked, curious about Hara, "Does Hara take after them?"

Anna cleaned her hands on a kerchief as she watched him wander around her shop. "Oh, yeah. But she's wary of her talent. Thanks to her dad."

He frowned and asked, "Her dad?"

Anna nodded. "Yeah. Stick around for a moment and I'll tell you all about him." Gideon watched as she put a kettle on and puttered around in the small room at the back of the post shop.

———◆———————◆———

Hara heard her Opa first. Crouched over the table, his elbow flapping as he screwed on the cover to a contraption. He picked up a small hammer to hit a stubborn corner into place.

This late, she would have expected him to be at dinner already.

Hara called, "Alfred? Opa."

The banging stopped, so he must have heard her, but when she went further into the workshop, he continued with his latest job.

He didn't turn but said to her, "Took you long enough. Your father came looking for you last year."

Hara shrugged. She really didn't want to talk about her father or the two years since she left him. "I decided to take the long way home. How was he?"

"Alive," he answered, blandly.

Hara winced when she asked the question. She had thought she had cut all her ties with her father after the scandal and betrayal. Alfred grunted, so nothing had changed with her father. She wandered over to his work and took a look.

Hara asked, "A sealed unit? What's it going to do?"

"It'll lift heavy objects with only one man's efforts."

That would be useful in this technology-sparse area. She helped him for a while and they were quiet as they worked.

Alfred asked, "You've been alright?"

Hara shrugged. "It's been alright. Better without dad."

He grunted in response. She added, "I kind of need your help. I have an airship which has some damage. You up to fixing it?"

His response was another grunt. That was all the answer she was going to get. They finished up and headed towards the ship. The sun had set and there wasn't a chance they would get any of the repairs done tonight.

Gideon leaned on the door outside the post shop. Hara looked past him to see if Anna was around but he was by himself. Alfred nodded his head in greeting and Gideon returned the gesture.

Alfred studied the airship from the ground. "You done a number to this girl, Hara, baby."

"Yeah, that's what happens when you run into pirates."

Her Opa gave her a sharp look, then turned back to the ship. "Crew?"

Hara shook her head. "We're a bit short-handed. I have some things I can do so we don't need as many crew as usual, but I'll need to pick up a few people as I go along. It was a close call with the pirates." Hara motioned to Gideon. "He sorted it out."

Alfred looked past her to Gideon, who had taken to standing behind her. "I owe you."

Gideon shrugged. "I did it for my own reasons."

That made Hara glance at the dragon. She kept forgetting he was a dragon and didn't have the same motivations as humans. She waved it off, because for the moment it didn't matter. She was free and alive. There were always options when you were free and alive. She had learnt that from her father. It wasn't the only thing, but it was the only thing she was proud of.

Hara changed the subject. "What can you do for the lady?"

Alfred grunted. It would be fixed in a day or two, judging by his face and grunt. He turned and started back to the workshop. "Come along. I have some stew and your room is still set up for you."

Hara trotted to keep up with her Opa's pace. "I've got a couple of people with me. Do you have enough space for them?"

Alfred shrugged. "Your father's room is free, but it's small."

Hara grinned. She remembered when they moved her father's room to the smaller room, and Alfred had given her the big room. Her father had been more than frazzled and his charm had been washed away with his confusion and anger.

Her large bed, which she made with Alfred, was decorated with old cogs from broken machines. That was when she knew that, despite his gruff nature, her Opa loved her. She had never been sure of her father's emotions towards her, but she didn't think love was one of them. Even though he often came to pick her up and take her on his travels, it was always for his benefit and not her own.

Halfway home, Henry came trotting out from between two buildings. He grinned as he said, "It's so good to be on good old terra firma." He waved to Alfred and asked, "Is this our mechanic?"

Hara motioned to Alfred. "This is my Opa. He's an engineer. He'll have the Blazing Blunderbuss up and running in no time."

Henry looked Alfred over. "You look familiar."

Alfred grinned. "Many say that. So, boy, are you part of my granddaughter's crew?"

Henry beamed. "Oh yeah, better than what I had before. I might actually get to cook for a living instead of shovelling coal."

Gideon said, "Good, because I hate cooking."

Hara chuckled. "That means you'll have to take his place at the boiler."

That made Gideon frown, and she smiled at the intense look on his face. It seemed her dragon wasn't up for much physical labour. She had already figured that out, but he was worth having along because he could turn into a sizable weapon at a moment's notice, and that was worth more than any amount of coal shovelling. It was a pity she would be taking him home soon.

⚜——————————⚜

Henry was in her father's room. Gideon had spoken to Alfred and apparently that had been the end of the sleeping arrangement argument. Hara stopped at the doorway to her room and stared at Gideon. "Are you mad?"

Gideon flicked his hair away from his face. "Many have commented that I am, but in my own opinion, I doubt they are the best judges of sanity."

Hara motioned to her room. "I don't think you get it. You can't share my room."

He shrugged, unperturbed by her aggressive tone. "I'll sleep on the floor. Do you have a pillow? I really like pillows. They can make the most awkward sleeping arrangements so much more comfortable."

She huffed and turned. She knew she wouldn't be able to convince him, and she wasn't up for a loud fight. Once in the room, she threw a pillow at him, followed by a blanket which was folded on the bottom of her bed. Her Oma had made it before she had died.

Gideon made himself a nest on the floor and he hummed as he worked. Hara shook her head. She wasn't surprised others thought he was crazy. He was a dragon and he was sleeping on the floor in her

43

bedroom. She tucked herself into her bed and dimmed the light, but sleep eluded her, and eventually she broke the silence. "You better not snore."

Gideon asked very seriously, "Is that the criteria for a man to share your room? That he doesn't snore."

She buried her face in her pillow, wishing she hadn't said anything. "It doesn't matter."

He was chatty as he asked, "Is there a list? A list would be very useful. Actually, I should make a list for you as well." He made a soft, contented sound and added, "A mate for me would have to be clever and brave. Definitely brave. I can't stand the simpering women at court. People think dragons want someone who is obsequious, but that only annoys most of us. Me included."

Hara wasn't sure when he had gotten the idea she should be his mate, but it made her uncomfortable. Connections were dangerous. They allowed people to use them with the excuse that it was for someone they loved. Anger roiled inside of her. She tamped it down, otherwise she wouldn't get any sleep at all.

There was a rustling sound and he continued talking. "I would want someone willing to get into trouble for me."

She groaned. That explained where he got the idea of her being his mate. "Is that why you've been following me around, because I was stupid enough to rescue you from those Roshian men?"

Gideon sounded very pleased when he made an assenting noise. She moved onto her elbow and looked down at him. Her eyes had adjusted to the darkness enough that she could make out his form on the floor, and he was lying on his back. She needed to set him straight before this got out of hand.

"Let me make something clear to you, dragon. I don't trust men. They're always trouble. They use you and then throw you away."

His head turned towards her. "Then it's a good thing I'm a dragon and not a man."

Hara flopped down and covered her head with her pillow. This was getting old very quickly. What was she supposed to do with a mad dragon? At least she would only have to deal with him for a short while. She would take him home and then she wouldn't have to think about him again.

Gideon waited for Hara to fall asleep before he got up. He wandered through the house. Alfred sat by the fire and didn't seem to be startled by Gideon's appearance. Alfred poured a drink and offered it to him. Gideon sat down with the drink though he didn't actually sip at it. They were quiet for a long while.

Eventually, Alfred asked, "Are you going to add her to your collection?"

Gideon wasn't surprised the old man recognised him as a dragon. Most who dealt with nobility knew the signs, and Alfred was someone Gideon recognised from a long time ago. Though he doubted the old man remembered him very well. "She is in my collection."

Alfred grunted. "Does she know that?"

Gideon grinned at the old man. "No, but that's part of the fun."

Alfred shook his head. "She's going to skin you alive when she finds out. Her old man has soured her towards men. The barnacles take him. He was his mother's favourite and she spoiled him rotten. I should never have let it happen. I made sure I did better with her. But you can't protect them from everything."

Gideon blinked at the tirade. Even when he had been an engineer in the Imperial Court, Alfred had never been a man of words. He had left that scene when he had married a woman well below his status and he hadn't wanted her to feel snubbed. At least, that was what the rumours said. Gideon knew more. Mildred had been an amazing engineer herself, but she hated crowds. While Alfred was the darling of the Court, his wife could never stay out of society. Alfred had given up his fame for his wife.

"I'll protect her," Gideon assured him.

Alfred took a sip of his drink as he thought. Gideon waited patiently. Even as a young man, Alfred had been worth listening to. Now he was older and probably wiser, Gideon was curious.

Eventually, Alfred said, "I think she needs someone who can be more than a protector. She's been hiding for too long. She could have come home and I could have protected her, but she wandered around. There was something she couldn't get from me."

Gideon propped his head on his hand and leant forward. "Really? Tell me what her life has been like."

Alfred raised an eyebrow. "She's a better engineer than me or Mildred."

Gideon recoiled a little and asked, "Really? Why, then, have we not heard of her? You know we like engineers. Gadgets interest us."

Alfred shrugged. "That's her father. He had her use her skills to defraud people. She's better known as Jeune in the influential circles. If they knew who she really was, they would hunt her down for what her father had done. I told you she is hiding. He would promise some marvellous things and say he had a new gadget which would make it all possible. He would have her make the gadget and then parade her and the gadget around. Once everyone had put in their investments, he would leave. Her gadgets are scattered all over the world; most collecting dust, as no one trusts them. She will never be safe if people know how good she is, so she will never fulfil her potential."

Gideon propped his chin again in his hand and thought about it for a long moment. After a while he said, "Do you think she enjoys travelling? She seems to have a soft spot for the airship. She doesn't have to have it fixed, after all. She could just stay here."

Alfred sat back and shrugged. "She doesn't fit here anymore. She figured that out before I did. A ship might be the place for her if she didn't have to hide who she was all the time."

Gideon nodded his head decisively. "Good. She can travel around and make her things and I'll make sure no one bothers her. That will make her happy."

Alfred asked, "What about you? I know you're not keen on human company. Will there be too many people travelling around like that?"

Gideon shrugged so Alfred did remember him from court. "It's the ones who keep dying. I hate that. It won't matter on a ship. People change too often for me to get attached. And I hate hanging around dragons, even if they don't keel over and die like humans do."

Alfred asked, "So you intend to bond with her?"

Gideon didn't hesitate before he answered. "Of course. But I'll build up to that. Where is the fun in rushing?"

Alfred just shook his head. The two of them finished their drinks in silence.

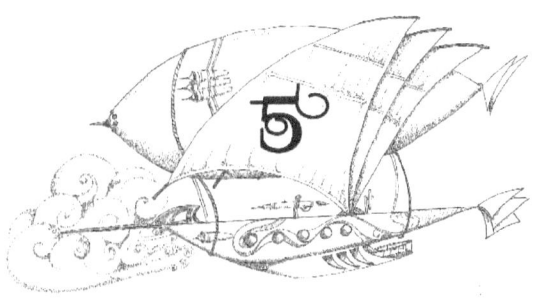

Hara asked Henry as she came out of her bedroom in the morning. "Have you seen Gideon?"

She had expected to see him still sleeping on her floor, but the bedding was packed away and there was no sign of him.

Henry shrugged and stuffed half an end of bread in his mouth before he left the house. She wasn't sure what he was off to see since the town was so small, but she wouldn't deny him the little freedom she could give him.

Her Opa had already packed up a case to work on the airship. She asked him, "Have you seen Gideon?"

Alfred grunted and lifted the pack over his shoulder and said, "Do you like him?"

Hara blinked at the blunt question. Then she sighed and said, "You're as bad as Anna. She thinks he's my beau."

"Well, isn't he?" he asked.

She shrugged, not in the mood to argue with anyone about the dragon. It seemed people jumped to conclusions no matter what she did. "I found him imprisoned by a couple of Rosh Barkers. I rescued him. Now he follows me like a puppy. That doesn't mean I like him. Any human being would try to help someone in that kind of situation."

She frowned as she looked around for him. "Or maybe not, as everyone seems to think there's more to it. That doesn't matter, anyway. Have you seen him?"

Alfred answered, "He said he was going to the tavern."

Hara sighed. That could be a dangerous thing. The regulars at the tavern were those who had too much money and not enough sense. They had workers making their money and spent most of the day swapping money with their fellow landowners in games of chance. None of them were of any real benefit to society. They certainly liked to talk brashly and often got into fights with visitors.

She headed towards the tavern, hoping she could prevent any disaster. The landowners would be almost ready to head home at this hour, as it was still early.

Hara was barely out of the workshop when one local stopped her. Hara sighed as Mr Hamlin, the butcher, looked her up and down. "You look very manly for a girl. What's your father been doing with you?"

She resisted the urge to punch him in the face. He was this rude to everyone, so he wasn't treating her any differently. "I haven't actually been with my father for the last few years."

That made him raise his eyebrows in concern—or was it censure instead? "Who's been looking after you, then?"

She rolled her eyes. "I'm twenty, Mr Hamlin. I don't need a keeper. Now, if you don't mind, I have to go rescue someone again."

Hara pushed past the man. This was why she couldn't stay with her Opa anymore. Everyone expected her to act like a girl. Well, maybe not her Opa, who had been the one to teach her how to be an engineer in the first place. But the others had thought it was not right.

When Hara was younger and had a crush on one of the farmer boys, he had been told by his parents that she wasn't suitable as a match. That was the story of her life. She wasn't suitable for a small town and she wasn't suitable to join the crowds who called themselves engineers. There was no place for her to belong to.

Hara looked at the airship floating above the small town and wondered if that was why she was thinking of keeping the ship. Maybe she could make a place where she could belong. Just like Henry, there were people who thought her choices in life had been wrong, but every choice had been about surviving. If only her life was as simple as choosing right over wrong. Most of her life she had only been given wrong choices to choose from.

Hara pushed open the door of the inn. She heard the commotion first before seeing in the dim light of the gas lamps a card table set up. The landlords laughed at something Gideon said. She came to stand behind him.

Gideon looked up at her and smiled. "Hello, beautiful."

She ignored the compliment. "What are you doing?"

He waved his cards to indicate the other landowners and said, "I'm taking their money."

Sir Jopsen grunted. "Hey, I'm not that far behind. Just give me a chance and I'll win it back."

Sir Mackay laughed. "You're so far in the hole, Jopsen. You'll soon need to take a loan from your mother-in-law." Everyone laughed at the comment, as Jopsen's mother-in-law was the one who held the purse strings, and they often teased the man about his limitations.

Gideon motioned to the pile of coins in front of him and said, "I started with a single copper."

Jopsen harrumphed. "And one we lent him."

Gideon grinned. "I'm good with numbers."

Mackay huffed, "He's a professor of maths, is what he is. He warned us when he sat down."

Jopsen said, "Not that we believed him until he won all our money."

Gideon threw in his cards. "I think my lady wants me, so I'm going to cash out." He scooped up the money into his shirt as there was too much to easily go into a pocket. The men muttered, but none of them complained that he was leaving the table with a small fortune.

Hara watched them cautiously to see if they would attack, and then remembered they weren't the usual men she dealt with. They weren't ruthless cads. Instead, they were small-time landowners who rarely moved their asses off their seats. She turned and followed Gideon as he left the inn.

Hara asked, "What were you doing here?"

Gideon waddled a little so he didn't spill his coins on the floor. "You don't have money. I thought you might need some. And since you aren't in my collection yet, you really need money of your own. While I have access to my own money I thought you would like some of your own."

Not that she was willing to take his winnings. He didn't understand that it was still his money even if he hadn't used his dragon magic to grab his coins from wherever dragons kept their hoard.

They stepped out of the tavern and stopped as they were surrounded by men. Heavily armed men. A man stepped out of the half-circle which surrounded them.

He said, "What the heck did you do to my baby?" It seemed the pirates had found them.

Gideon asked, "Was it really your baby? I mean, you left it guarded with a single crewman and a prisoner. It was almost like you were asking for it to be stolen. I mean, you were sitting in a smugglers' port. Everyone there has some experience in stealing."

The man glared at Gideon. "And you think that gives you leave to take off with my ship? My busted-up ship, thanks to you."

Hara stepped forward a little, hoping to prevent the pirates from shooting the dragon, and said, "No need to get upset. I'm sure we can come to an arrangement."

Gideon brightened. "Of course. Money. I have money. Why don't we buy your ship? Pay for your travels here, and you can go away and buy a new ship and everyone's happy."

The pirate said, "It isn't as simple as that. But I'm interested. Who wants a busted-up ship, anyway? They're never right, even after repairs."

Gideon grinned. "Excellent."

Hara put her hand on his arm. "Gideon, you can't be serious."

He turned to her. "Of course, this is perfect. You can be a captain and you don't have to live here."

What did he mean by that? The pirate captain said, "It isn't going to be cheap."

Gideon shrugged. "How about we start with this?"

He poured the coins from his shirt onto the ground. All the pirates' eyes followed the dropping money.

Gideon clapped his hands excitedly. "Good, it looks like we can negotiate."

The pirate captain snapped up his head. "I want three times that for the ship, and I want all that in gold coins for the trouble you've put us through."

Hara gaped. That was more than what a rich noble would gain in a year from the rents of his peasants.

Gideon surprised her when he said, "Done."

He twisted his hand in the air and more coins joined the ones on the ground until it made a mound which came up to her knees. The captain motioned to one of his men and they shovelled the coins into a bag.

The captain came closer and said, "There are some things you need to know about the ship. She is a privateer. A Rosh ship. They financed her."

Hara frowned at the captain. "So she isn't even your ship to sell?"

He shrugged. "Oh, she was mine. I just got a little into hock with the wrong people. I'm afraid that debt goes with the ship. The Rosh don't particularly care who is flying her. Or you can see if they forget about her and leave you alone. We'll go collect our gear. Nice doing business with you." He tipped his hat as a farewell.

Hara didn't like this development. The pirates packed up the last of the coins. They disappeared as quickly as they appeared. She turned to Gideon now that they were alone.

Hara hit his arm. "Thanks. Now I have a pirate ship."

Gideon was completely oblivious to her sarcasm as he grinned. "You are welcome."

She glared at him. "You don't get it. The Rosh are now going to be after us."

He tilted his head to the side, reminding her of an animal. He asked, "Weren't we being chased by Rosh people already so more Rosh people won't really make a difference in the long run?"

Hara threw her hands up in frustration and walked away. She was an idiot to try to talk rationally with a dragon.

Gideon asked, "Where are you going?"

She threw the comment over her shoulder, "To fix my new airship, apparently. Though technically it is yours."

"Nonsense. What would I want with an airship? I have my own wings. Consider it payment for saving my life. Or we can settle it completely if you agree to be in my collection."

Hara snorted. "In your dreams Gideon."

He purred, "Mm, my dreams. Sweetheart, you will always be in my dreams."

Hara blushed, but decided silence was a better solution to his annoying presence.

———————————

Hara passed the wrench up to Alfred. He grunted as a thank you and she went back to putting together the join, which he would replace once he had installed the sail mast.

Alfred asked, "Why did you leave your father? I mean, you have always stuck by him."

Hara wasn't astonished that he was confused by her loyalty to her father. She said, "You mean even after he was such a douche bag. Well, the last time he left me, to be honest, and that was in a prison. That was the last straw. When I ended up in the court, the judge took pity on me or I would still be there. He put me to work on a ship and once I paid my time I started back, but I just never quite got here until now."

Hara sighed and added. "I don't fit here, Opa. I don't know if I fit anywhere."

Alfred grunted, but he didn't disagree. He finished the attachment and waved his hand and she passed him the next thing.

He asked, "You want anything special put on your ship? She is yours, after all."

Hara sighed. "You know he bought it for me. Do I owe him anything for that? I'm not sure how owing and debt work with him."

Her Opa stopped for a moment and looked at her with a quizzical look. After a moment, he asked, "You know he is a dragon, right?"

Hara was shocked. "Yeah, but I didn't think anyone else knew."

Alfred shrugged. "It is the eyes. Though most dragons are usually bigger. They can choose their form when they arrive on this plane. Most wanted to intimidate. He was different. From a different faction, I reckon. I never got the whole story. But dragons have golden eyes."

Hara blinked in stunned confusion and she eventually asked, "You knew him? Before, I mean. I knew dragons could live for a very long time. I mean, he doesn't look that old." She winced at her babbling.

Her Opa didn't seem to care about her rambling and nodded. "He used to hang around the court when I was there."

Hara had known her Opa had once been a famous engineer, but she had always assumed it had only been around other engineers. She had never thought of him brushing shoulders with dragons and nobles.

Alfred went back to installing the join and she asked, "What was he like back then?"

His face screwed up and he stuck his tongue out between his teeth as he worked. He finished installing the piece and he eventually said, "A geek. He likes numbers more than he likes people or even other dragons."

Why wasn't she surprised by that? But if he was a dragon who visited court and probably had a lot of money, what was he doing hanging out with her?

"So why did he buy me an airship?"

Alfred shrugged. "I wouldn't worry about it. Dragons don't see money the same way we do. Gold is only useful to them once they have found a mate. Before that, they see it as a useful thing to collect but not particularly valuable. It is too common to be a treasure in their collection. They like the rare and unattainable for their collections. Money is neither of those for them. You don't owe him anything."

Hara huffed. She didn't like not knowing the dragon's thoughts on it all. "Nobody does something like that without expecting something in return."

Alfred stopped and looked at her for a long moment before he said, "What do you think of him?"

She shrugged. "He is annoying. He always hangs around and he talks all the time. He flirts with me. He is just annoying."

Alfred grunted and went back to work. After a while, he asked, "Are you ever going to settle down with a man?"

She was shocked by the question, as her Opa he had never been one to ask about her love life. This wasn't the first time that day he had asked either. Why was he so concerned all of a sudden about what she thought about the dragon? He had never cared before about her love life. Actually, anything which had to do with being a girl had been too difficult for him to talk about. It had been Anna who informed her how to deal with her period and other girly things.

Hara peered past the gears so she could see his face, but he continued to work as if the words he had said were innocuous. She sighed. "I'm only starting to figure out what I want from life without complicating it with a man."

Her Opa stopped and Alfred pushed out from under the contraption he was working on. He looked at her for a long moment, then said, "I hoped that seeing how happy Mildred and I were that you would see there can be a joy in being with someone who understands you."

Hara sighed. "I saw that, but Opa, I'm a smart woman and I can get through life without a man if I wanted to."

Alfred raised a single eyebrow. "I didn't say anything about you being able to live without a man. I mean, there is happiness you can get with someone else you can't have by yourself."

Hara snorted. "I'm happy as I am now. I don't need a man to be happy."

He frowned at her words, then shook his head. "Just don't chase away people who want to be in your life, sweetheart. You might regret it."

She certainly regretted sticking by her father for so long. She could do without this happiness her Opa talked about if it meant having to put up with the downs as well.

At least now, with her ship fixed, she could take the dragon home.

Hara looked down when a woman called. "Hey, there."

The woman was dressed in grey, drab clothes. Hara looked at her Opa but he waved her off. She climbed down the scaffold to the ground.

The girl stood with her hands twisted in her skirts. Hara asked, "Yeah?"

The girl hesitated, then asked, "I hear you need a hand with your ship here."

Hara looked the girl up and down and then leant against the scaffolding and asked, "What is your story?" Because there had to be one for a girl of good family to want to sign on with a ship like hers.

Though the girl was plainly dressed, she had a ribbon in her hair and ink stains on her fingers. She had been educated, higher than most women were educated and her family had enough money to occasionally buy a small luxury like ribbons. Her clothes were practical and plain, but the cloth was thick and well woven. Anyone who signed on with her would lose whatever reputation they had.

The girl sighed. "I'm not from a rich family. My father is a third generation farm worker. But I grew up pretty close to one of the landowner families. They aren't particularly rich either, but they have a nice little farm. Well, they have a son. And I thought he was sweet on me."

Hara sighed. She had heard this story too many times. "I get it. Now, he isn't interested in you anymore?"

She shook her head, blushing profusely. "No, it isn't exactly what you think. You see, when I told him no, he started telling everyone I was easy and available. Even if I wanted to make a match, no one will have me as they think I sleep with landowners for money. I just need to get out of here. Find a place for myself where people don't know me."

Hara tapped her chin with her finger as she thought. They were short-handed but they really needed skilled people. It was not conventional to take on a female crew. But people would have to get used to it if Hara was to remain the captain.

Hara asked, "Are you willing to work?"

She nodded her head vigorously.

Hara gave in. "Then meet back here tomorrow. We will leave just after dawn."

The girl's face lit up and she grabbed Hara's hand before shaking it vigorously. "You won't regret this, Captain." She turned and trotted away, excited.

Hara called out before the girl was too far away. "What is your name?"

The girl turned and said, "I'm Alice." She skipped backwards and spun around and trotted away.

A darn puppy is what Alice reminded her of. She would probably be as bad as the blasted dragon. Taking in strays, as she did, would quickly lead to trouble.

———————

Hara helped the new girl up onto the ship. Henry eyed Alice as she climbed up the ladder. The girl looked around and then picked up her single bag and went further into the ship. The ship was a little messed up as the pirates hadn't been particularly careful when they had cleaned out their things the day before.

Henry turned to Hara and asked, "Who is the girl?"

Hara pulled up the gear and grunted as she pulled it over the lip of the deck. "That is the new crewmember, Alice, and no, you are not to chase her. She has had enough trouble here in town. She doesn't need a sex starved work mate chasing after her."

Henry ducked his head and blushed. "Wasn't thinking to."

Hara turned to him. "Good, because this is not a pirate ship and so there will be no raping and pillaging."

He huffed. "Not that they let me off the ship when they were taking on others."

Hara raised an eyebrow and asked, "What are you more upset about? That you couldn't rape and pillage or get off the ship?"

61

Henry wrinkled his nose. "Sorry, I'm just mad. I'm still stuck on this blasted ship."

She said, "There is no need for you to stay."

Henry shook his head. "There is. I don't have anywhere else to go."

She thought about that for a moment. "You were a cook. If you could get a job in a tavern or something, would you be happy with that?"

He shrugged, suddenly shy to speak to her. She raised her eyebrows. "I know places where no one will care who you were on a pirate ship and that you had to turn to survive. Don't worry, you will be landlocked soon enough."

Gideon pulled himself up the ladder and thumped down heavily as he threw his legs over the low railing where the ladder was. He grinned at her. "Morning, beautiful."

She glared at him. "Don't call me beautiful."

He asked without hesitation. "Oh, would sweetheart be better?"

Hara rolled her eyes and walked away. Hopefully, if she ignored his flirting, he would stop. Though she wouldn't hold her breath.

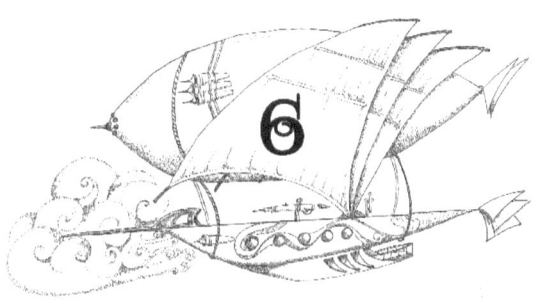

Gideon leant against the window and looked outside. He said, "Where are we going?"

Hara set their course and said distractedly. "I'm taking you home."

He spun around and looked at her. "I thought I told you I would like to stick with you for a while."

She shrugged and added, "And I don't particularly care what you want."

Gideon stepped closer so she was forced to look up into his face. Though he wasn't a tall man he was taller than her. His golden eyes sparked with his frustration. He did not look like his usually amused and distracted self. "If I wanted to return to my abode, I would have said as much."

Hara raised an eyebrow, curious by this change in him. "Just be happy you are getting a free ride. It is the least I can do after you used your winnings to buy the ship."

He growled and it was so much like an animal growl that it made her eyes widen in shock. But she wasn't about to be intimidated. "I am heading for the capital of the Empire and you said you would tag along. Well, mate, you are going to tag along until we get there and then we can go our separate ways."

His gold eyes sparked and he turned away. "We will see."

She didn't think she had won this argument, but at least it was over for the moment.

Alice coughed from the doorway and asked, "Should I come back later?"

Hara shook her head and motioned for the girl to approach. "I need to teach you how to do a few things so you can help me on the bridge. Gideon is all but useless."

He snorted to show he had heard but wasn't going to be insulted. He wouldn't be that easy to be rid of.

Hara brought Alice over to the map. "This is where we are now. This is where we are heading. Guess the plot we might take."

The girl studied the map for a moment and it told Hara the girl was conscientious. Eventually, she traced a finger over the map. She said, "You'd want to avoid the mountains."

Hara smiled, pleased with her comment. "Yes. We have a certain amount of lift, but we are buoyant static at the moment and even with compensators we wouldn't be able to cross those peaks."

Alice's finger stopped on a town and she asked, "Will we stop along the way?"

Hara shifted a piece of sheer paper over the map to show their planned route. They would go through the town the girl had pointed out. "By law, we have to. These towns are called border towns. We need to stop there to get our papers signed. Hopefully, we can also pick up cargo as money is in short supply."

Alice said absently as she continued to study the map. "I like numbers."

Hara laughed. "Then you will get on with Gideon."

Alice looked up with some confusion, but Hara didn't clarify. Maybe if Hara could guide the dragon's attention to someone else who was better suited to him, he would forget about her. Men had been like that before. Hopefully the dragon was as equally fickle.

───────────────

The border town had mine balloons floating off to either side of the town. Forcing airships to funnel through the town. Hara watched the men on towers with flags motioning for her to take up a position in a queue of airships.

The town would be their last stop before they entered the Empire. It would be a good place to pick up supplies and maybe cargo. It would be best to find work so she wouldn't have to rely on Gideon and his gambling skills.

Alice asked, "Will it be safe?"

Hara glanced over her shoulder at the girl and thought about her question seriously. Border towns like this usually held a unique kind of riffraff.

Hara pulled a knife from her boot and passed it to the girl. "The first thing you should always do is run. But if that isn't an option, use the knife. Now you should be alright."

Alice eyed the knife for a moment before she took it and tucked it into her own boot beneath her skirts. Hara would have to get the girl some clothes, which would work better on the ship than bulky skirts. She planned to take the first shift on the Airship and install some things she made in the last week of travel.

Hopefully, with her improvements, they could actually fight back if they were ever attacked. She couldn't completely automate the guns, but she had rerouted them and made it so she could shoot all the guns from the bridge. With Alice on the bridge as well, they might even have a slim chance the next time they were attacked by pirates.

Hara glanced over at Gideon. He had sulked the last week and it annoyed her. Couldn't he argue with her like a normal person? When they docked and the others left, Gideon remained.

He came to stand by her. "I'm not going to go. You will have to get used to that."

She hauled out the equipment she intended to install and asked, "And why is that?"

Gideon looked thoughtful. He didn't answer her. Instead he asked, "What do you know about dragons and their collections?"

Her Opa had spoken about dragons, but she had never been very interested in finding anything out about them. She had always thought they were man-eating monsters, so what was the point of finding out more of them?

Hara glanced at him and shrugged. "Nothing really. You guys are obsessed with your collections, is all I know."

He cocked up an eyebrow which went up into his long fringe. She really wanted to give him a haircut. His half-cocked smiled, went with the eyebrow annoyed her as he said, "It is more than that. We gain our status from what we have collected. The more we can look after, the more status we have. The more unique our collection is, differentiates our status at the higher levels of rank."

Hara frowned at him for a moment and he continued. "If you have an extensive collection, you would have a rank like in an army unit of colonel. To be considered a general, you would have to have something unique in your collection."

She asked, suspicious of his motives or the validity of his words. "And you think women should be in your collection?"

He frowned until there was a wrinkle on his nose. "We look after those in our collection. I know people think it is slavery, but it is more like servitude."

Hara snorted and went back to her work. She said snidely, "Like servitude is better than slavery."

Gideon frowned and then clicked his fingers as he figured something out. "Not your slavery or servitude, Hara, but rather ours. I mean dragons. Once you are in a collection, you are served by the dragon. We choose carefully who is worthy to be in our collection as it might mean our lives."

She turned and blinked at him in astonishment. After a long moment, she asked, "Your servitude? So you don't want me to belong to you?"

Gideon looked confused before he said, "Yes, I do, but not as a slave."

Hara frowned and he explained, waving his hands around to add to his words. "Like with your Opa. You went to him to get the ship fixed as you knew he would do it without question. You belong to him so he serves you."

Hara had never been accused of being a dimwit so she finally understood what he tried to explain. "Oh, bugger, you want to be family."

Gideon grinned, happy he had finally convinced her. "Exactly, but dragons, we are hatched and none of our females or males have attachments to their young. We do not have families in the same way humans do. We collect family though and I want to be in your family."

Hara stopped and leant on the wrench she was using. She studied the dragon for a long while. There was a flaw in his logic. He might choose his family, but she couldn't.

Eventually she said, "I have my own family and they would be your family as well."

Gideon nodded. "I'm aware of this. Your Opa is worthy."

If only her Opa were the only family she had left. "But you haven't met my father."

Gideon frowned. "If you are his child, then he should be worthy."

He really needed to study humans more. She snorted and went back to work. She said as she put in the console to fire the weapons from. "I won't be in your collection, Gideon, until you have met my father."

There was a long silence from the dragon and she looked to see what he was doing.

Gideon thought and eventually said, "I have seen this tradition amongst humans. I agree to this stipulation."

She wasn't about to ask what he meant by that and went back to work. Maybe if he thought she was willing to join his collection, he would leave her alone to work peacefully for a short time. Besides, she really didn't think he would find her father worthy.

Hara said, "Fine. Now can you pass me that console front, please?"

He passed it to her. "You know you wouldn't need the guns if you kept me around."

Hara laughed. "I'm still going to take you back to the capital, Gideon. I know you won't find my father worthy so we might as well end things sooner rather than later."

Hara trolled the inns to see if she could find cargo for the Blazing Blunderbuss. She hadn't had any luck, but there was one thing she had discovered. She would need a male agent to work through as when they found out she was not a hussy, they weren't interested in talking to her about any business.

It could have all gone particularly messy if Gideon hadn't tagged along. Though he hadn't done anything, usually they would look over her shoulder at him and they would back down. She didn't think they knew he was a dragon but the threat of a male, even a scholar like the dragon, was enough to make them behave.

Hara jumped back when someone was thrown out of the door of the inn in front of her.

Gideon peered over at the man. "You alright there, mate?"

The man got up and dusted himself off before he said, "I'm fine. Just a disagreement about how much I was owed."

He steeled himself and threw himself back into the bar. Hara shook her head. She only came across these kinds of people in border towns like this one.

Hara turned when she heard someone call out to Gideon.

A large man leaned against a nearby wall. The two of them approached the man. Gideon grinned and shook the man's hand. Clearly, he recognised the man.

"Patrick, what are you doing here? You never like to leave your hometown."

Patrick shrugged. "I had some things to see to. My ships have been attacked consistently on their way to Ming so I thought I would come and see what the problem is myself."

Patrick frowned at Gideon, "I didn't think I would see you here. You usually stick around different university campuses."

Gideon motioned to Hara. "I got into some trouble, but Hara here rescued me."

Patrick took a long moment to study her. He then turned back to Gideon and asked, "So, are you heading home?"

Gideon wrinkled his nose. "She insists."

Hara glared at Gideon. But neither of the men seemed to notice her sharp look.

Patrick stood up from the wall. "Come have some lunch. I might have a job for you. I need something taken to the guild council in the capital."

Gideon turned to her, but she shook her head. She had to find crew for them, otherwise it would be pointless to get cargo as they wouldn't be going anywhere.

Hara said, "Spend time with your friend. I'll meet you back at the ship. I have to find some more crew, anyway."

Gideon shrugged. "As long as you miss me."

She rolled her eyes and walked away. She could hear Patrick asking. "Is that your lady?"

Gideon announced loud enough she heard him even over the crowd as she walked away. "She will be."

Hara wasn't ready to be owned by anyone, let alone an annoying dragon like Gideon.

Hara headed for the guildhall, hoping a border town like this had men to spare who would be worth their pay. Though so far she hadn't paid anyone as she still had no coin to pay them until she finished a delivery. She had scraped what she could together and had Alice and Henry buy what supplies they could. She knew she could ask Gideon, but she didn't like digging herself deeper into that kind of trouble.

The guild hall was dingy and she wrinkled her nose at the smell of ale and stale sweat. She walked over to the hiring book and didn't look at anyone. They might assume she was here for a different reason than to hire someone for her airship and hopefully leave her alone.

She had only just flipped the page when a crash made her look over her shoulder. A man chased something around the room and careened into tables. She assumed it was a rat or something as the man picked up a broken chair leg and battered at something hidden under a tipped over table.

Hara turned back to the hiring book. She didn't want to know just how big the rat was, that the man had to go so vigorously after it to kill it. She wrote the names of a few men who looked promising. She would have to meet them first to see if they would take orders from a woman.

Something zipped past her head and Hara ducked. The man with the broken chair leg slammed into the podium and her. They all went down in a tumble.

Hara swore at the idiot and shoved at him until he was off her and she could get to her feet. The man also swore and then lunged at something which was perched on the downed podium.

She now saw it was no rat. Instead, it was a clockwork creature shaped like a small dragon. When the man lunged, it made a twittering sound and lunged into the air. It spread out wings made of brass and thin leather parchment.

It landed on her shoulder and its little claws dug in as it scurried behind her neck and under her braided hair.

The man went to swing at her but she grabbed the chair leg and pulled it out of his grip. She bared her teeth at the idiot. "Leave it. Go back to your ale."

The drunk man glared at her. A voice from one of the few standing tables echoed through the room. "He has been chasing that for half an hour. Upstairs and now downstairs."

Hara turned to look at the man who had spoken. He sat with his feet up on the table and casually held an ale in his hand.

He added. "I have money on him not killing it." He motioned to some of the other men in the room. "They bet he could squish it to smithereens."

Hara rolled her eyes. Aircrew could bet on anything, even something as silly as smashing up a clockwork creature. She knew a little more about the creature and knew smashing it would be a mistake.

She turned back to the idiot. "Do you have any money on it?"

He snarled. "A whole Guinea."

Hara dug into a pocket and flicked him two Guineas. The creature was worth a heck of a lot more. But she cringed at handing over any of her resources. The idiot shrugged and sauntered off. Probably to get drunk. He would have worn off a bit of his buzz with all the running around and would be in need of a top up.

Once he was gone, she looked for the piece of paper which had the names she had collected before. The man who had helped her out before asked, "Can I help you?"

Hara turned and looked at him. He had large knives strapped all over his body. He was also a big man. She asked, "Are you here looking for work?"

He lifted a shoulder in a non-committal gesture. "I could do with work, but my last job made me wish for a very long holiday."

She looked him up and down. He was a fighter, clear as day. She could do with a bit of muscle. She asked, "Would you take orders from a woman?"

"Only women who aren't idiots."

She chuckled at his comment. "Well, I'm not one of those. Come check out the Blazing Blunderbuss. If you like the armament, you can sign on."

The man studied her for a long moment. "No need to check her out. You can always upgrade armament, but you can't get upgrade a bad captain."

The creature on her shoulder moved and tightened its tail around her neck. Hara reached up and stroked its head. She said to her new crew member. "You are not wrong there. If we don't mesh, I'll make sure you get to a decent city rather than a dump like this place."

He nodded. "Fair enough." He offered his hand to shake on the deal. "Murphy is the name. Guns are my game."

She returned the gesture and shook his hand. "I'm Hara and I think we'll get along."

———————————————

After everyone had settled Patrick's cargo in the hold, Hara sent Gideon to settle in Murphy while she checked in with Alice. Henry was to procure supplies and she was worried as he hadn't checked in with them yet.

Alice asked, "What is that?"

The clockwork dragon peeked out from her collar and trilled softly. Alice snatched back her finger, which had been close to touching the creature and held it close to her chest. She asked timidly. "Is it going to bite me?"

Gideon sauntered on to the bridge. "What have you two in a tizzy? I've settled the new guy. He likes the guns, by the way." He hissed when he saw the creature and asked, "Why the heck did you bring that thing here?"

Hara, pleased she had ruffled Gideon's feathers, said, "Don't worry. You won't be here long enough for it to annoy you. This is a clockwork dragon."

Gideon snarled and the creature bared its teeth back at him.

Alice asked Gideon, "Is it dangerous?"

Gideon snorted. "Hardly. It is just metal and wires."

Hara chuckled. "A little more than that. This is an example of the first successful artificial intelligence. It isn't very smart. More like a bird or something. But it can mimic what it sees. I've only ever seen one before and it had cost the lord a fortune." She stroked the creature's head. "They wander off if they don't like their master. Isn't that right, little one? You and I are going to be best buds."

Gideon huffed. "I'm going to my room." Alice and Hara watched him storm off.

Alice asked, "Do you think he will be alright?"

Hara shrugged. "He is just in a snit. He will get over it. Maybe he'll be happy about going home now."

Alice shrugged. She didn't look convinced. Hara noticed then that was Alice prepared to leave the ship as she was wearing her coat.

Hara frowned. "Are you going somewhere?"

Alice said, "Henry isn't back yet."

"Yeah, I noticed. I'll go look for him. I just wanted to make sure everything was all right here. Can you monitor the boys? Murphy seems harmless enough."

Alice chuckled, "Really? When I saw him, he looked like he was an advertisement for a weapons store."

Hara shook her head. "No, he is just a big boy who likes his toys. He didn't even check out my breasts or snicker when I had a large man lying all on top of me."

When Alice gave her a shocked look, Hara waved it off and said, "Another story for another day. You can always ask Murphy. He will probably tell you a more elaborate and amusing version."

Alice chuckled at the idea. "Not to worry, I will keep the home fires burning."

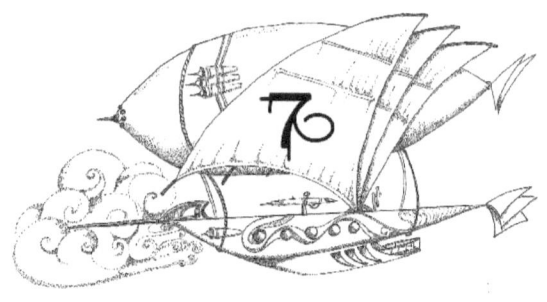

When Hara got to the market area, she saw the vendors were mostly packed up for the day. She frowned. Henry wouldn't have stuck around after the market had closed.

She heard someone yell and some wood crack as someone was thrown into a crate. She ran towards the sound. As Hara rounded the corner into the alley, she was shocked by the tableau.

Henry was on the ground and there were two other men fighting on the other end of the alleyway. She had no idea who they were but it seemed the fight was winding down. Hara approached and helped Henry to his feet. The fight was over by the time she had helped dust off Henry.

The man left standing was a big bruiser of a man. He approached Hara, rubbing his jaw where he obviously had been hit. He asked Henry, "You alright?"

Henry nodded. "Yeah, thanks."

The bruiser offered his hand to her. She took it and asked, "I take it you came to the rescue of my cook?"

The man said, "He was lured here by a few men. I thought I would even up the odds."

Hara looked past the man and saw there were indeed a few unconscious and groaning men. She pursed her lips, briefly impressed with the man's fighting skills and said, still looking at the carnage. "Do you need a job?"

The man grunted. "I need to get out of town. Does that count?"

Hara turned back to him. "We can work with that. I'm Captain Hara. You've met Henry."

He ran a hand through his hair as he said, "I'm Kale."

"Well, Kale, if you are ready, we really should leave. We are heading towards the capital and I hope that gets you far enough away from any of your enemies." Hara could do with more crew even if they were only temporary.

Kale jumped and she assumed the clock work dragon had moved to her shoulder. He had been looking right at her and now his eyes were directed to her shoulder.

Hara said, "Don't mind him. She doesn't bite." Kale looked skeptical.

Henry said, "That is new. Has Gideon seen it?"

Hara smiled and turned to Henry. "Yeah, and they hit it off like oil and water." She stroked the dragon and it settled again.

Henry eyed it curiously. "Does it just stay there?"

"Sure. It seems comfortable." It probably liked being able to see new things. It also had the bonus of annoying people.

Hara called out to the rest as she moved from the deck further into the ship. "Hey guys, we are back and we brought a friend."

When they got to the bridge, Alice and Murphy were there.

Henry waved back to Kale. "Meet Kale. He saved my life."

Alice came up behind Hara and whispered, "He looks massive."

Kale grinned suggestively and must have super human hearing as he added, "It is all muscle." He flexed his arm to demonstrate.

Henry missed the suggestive tone towards Alice and added excitedly, "Yeah, without him I would have been beaten to a pulp."

Hara rolled her eyes. "I think you have been living amongst pirates for too long, Henry." She motioned to the ship in general. "We'll need a few hands to stoke the fires and trim sails."

Henry hesitated, then said, "I'll go make dinner."

Hara waved off Henry and said to the others when they gave her a look to see who would have the unwanted chore of shovelling coal. "Well, I'm hungry already and he has had his fair share of ship work lately."

Murphy said, "Fine, I'll go flex my muscles. Come along, new guy, I'll show you the ropes."

Once they had left, Alice approached Hara. "I don't like the new guy, Kale. He looks at me a certain way."

Hara looked at Alice with concern. "Come here. I want to show you something."

Alice had come from a sheltered upbringing. It was time to teach her how to look after herself when around men who didn't know their manners. Hara had given her the knife and now it was time to show her how to use it and other less lethal methods when dealing with a stronger force. Hara wished Alice would be safe in any circumstances, but she knew from experience that wasn't true.

Hara reached up to the dragon on her shoulder and tapped a paw and pointed it at the wheel. It chirped and glided from her shoulder to perch on the wheel.

Alice asked as she watched the small creature, "It can fly?"

Hara glanced back at the dragon. "Not really. It can glide a bit. It weighs too much to truly fly. It is a clever creation, but really it is only a novelty. Now let me show you how to use that knife."

Alice was still distracted. "Are you going to name it?"

Hara grinned, she had thought of a name on the way back to the Blazing Blunderbuss. "I already did. Her name is Angel."

Alice brought her attention away from the dragon. "That is pretty."

"I know. Maybe a little too pretty when Gideon hears." There was amusement in Hara's voice.

Alice asked, confused. "Gideon? Why would he not like the name?"

"Gideon is an angel's name. It will annoy the heck out of him." Hara enlightened.

Alice sighed and shook her head lightly. "I don't know why you and Gideon can't get along. He is a rather nice man."

That made Hara interested. "Has Gideon been flirting with you?"

"No. You know he is sweet on you, don't you?" Alice asked, confused.

"Yeah, and that is part of the problem." Hara didn't want to explore her feelings for the dragon. They, at the very least, were complicated.

Alice frowned, but didn't ask any more. Hara couldn't explain that it was all the more complicated because Gideon wasn't everything he seemed to be and she really didn't want hysterical people when they found out that they had a dragon on board. The sooner they dropped him off at home, the better.

———————————

Hara set the food down in front of Gideon where he sat on the bridge. "Henry said it is a simple stew, but it smells better than anything I've made." They had the watch and she hadn't done anything to change the schedule. Gideon might annoy her, but he was still good company on watch while everyone else was asleep.

Gideon put out some plates. He seemed to not mind doing any servant work. She would have thought the haughty dragon would expect others to wait on him. He pulled out her chair.

Angel chirped as she had been sleeping on the chair. Gideon growled at her. But she seemed unperturbed and scuttled to find another place to sleep.

Hara eyed the plates. "Those are real china. Are you sure you want to use those?"

Gideon blinked at her in confusion. "They are lovely and you insist this will be our last night together so I would like to use something that is as lovely as you."

"I don't want to argue, Gideon." Hara sighed.

He glanced at her. "Who is arguing?"

She sat down in the chair he offered. "I just don't want anything to be broken. We are in a moving vehicle. Things can get broken."

Hara was nervous, but she couldn't put her finger on why.

Gideon said, "We could have this every night, you know."

Hara knew he wasn't talking about the nice china or the food. She ate something so she wouldn't say anything. She had dreamed of this when she was younger, but then it had turned bitter when she realised she was destined to end up with someone like her father. After all, everyone said you married someone like your father. The nice dinner every blue moon was not worth the trouble in between.

Gideon raised an eyebrow and then chattered about random things. She smiled softly as she ate. She would miss him and that bothered her more than she wanted to admit.

———————

Y ou don't have to be such a baby about it. You are home and it is better that way." Hara said as they dodged people on the street. Angel chirped from her shoulder, mimicking her as closely as she could.

Gideon glared at her, but still followed as he continued to argue. "It is you who needs maturity. You fear me and what I will do to change your life, therefore you wish to rid yourself of me."

Hara didn't look back as she answered. "You are not wrong."

He huffed. "Then, if you agree you are the juvenile in this situation, why are you making me stay here?"

She hated he was being logical and said honestly, "I need time."

Gideon caught her arm and made her turn. He studied her face for a long moment, then said, "I do not think so. I spoke to your grandfather and he says you have been travelling for years. You do not need time, you need to face your fears."

Hara raised an eyebrow and asked, "And you reckon you are the one fear I should face?"

"Yes," he said gleefully. Angel chirped an agreement and Gideon grinned at the small creature.

Hara glared at Angel and whispered, "Traitor." She was tired of this conversation. "Let us get to your place and we can talk about this in private." She spun on her heel and continued to move through the crowds as fast as they would allow her.

Gideon said, "I'm aware you're still going to leave me behind. I haven't convinced you. You hide even from yourself and this is not healthy."

She threw over her shoulder as she pushed through the crowds. "And you don't hide? Alfred told me a little about you. That you don't like dragons and you spend most of your time amongst humans? What are you afraid of? A bit kettle calling the pot black, don't you think?"

When he didn't answer, she looked over at him. His gold eyes were dark with his emotions. Maybe it would be best to leave this conversation where it was.

They arrived at the address she had wheedled out of him earlier. His home was a large building of apartments. Hara was astonished Gideon didn't live in a mansion. She had thought all dragons were rich. After all, he had dropped a fortune on that pirate to buy the airship and he hadn't even blinked.

Gideon said, "Are you going to come up?"

Hara sighed and took her attention away from the building. Angel chirped, asking as well. The clockwork dragon was fairly easy to understand as she changed the tones of her chirps.

Hara said, "I'll have to. Otherwise, you will just follow me back and I promised you we would talk."

He flashed her a grin and waved for her to lead the way. She said as they entered the elevator. "You need to stay away from me. I'm only trouble."

So maybe the building was a little more posh than it looked outside. Only rich places could afford to put in elevators. Gideon leant against the wall of the elevator and watched her. Hara tried her best to ignore him.

Instead, she asked, "What are you going to do now?"

His gold eyes sparked with interest and she blushed and said, "No, I mean when I'm gone."

He chuckled. "Pine away."

Angel seemed concerned for Gideon and made a noise to show that. Hara patted Angel to reassure her. "He'll be fine, Angel."

Gideon denied that. Placing a hand over his heart and pretended to be wounded. "You can't be sure. Maybe the next time you see me, I will have wasted away."

Hara rolled her eyes and prayed for the elevator to reach his floor. The doors pinged and opened. She rushed out and Gideon chuckled at her haste. A large foyer led into several rooms.

It took her a moment to realise there was only one apartment on the entire floor. So maybe having an apartment was actually not so cheap after all. She stopped, though, when she saw two men standing in the centre of the sitting room.

Gideon was saying something to her, but stopped when he saw the men. If he were a dog, she would have said his hackles rose.

Gideon's tone changed to hostile. "What are you doing here?"

The taller of the two men said, "I'm here by the will of the Emperor."

"He isn't my Emperor." Gideon snapped. She wondered if they were speaking about the Emperor of the Empire or some dragon equivalent.

The other man interjected before Gideon could start on a rant. "We don't have time for this. Gideon, we have come here to tell you that your life is in danger. There is a group of Rosh Barkers looking for you."

Hara snorted. The two men looked at her and the tall one stalked up to her. Gideon stepped between her and the man. "She is mine."

She wasn't going to argue as the man was a beast and she didn't like the way he looked at her. So she would be a coward and hide behind Gideon's possession.

The way they reacted to each other suggested this new man was a dragon. He certainly had the size for it. He was taller than she realised, as the other man he had been standing next to was equally tall for the human species. Maybe he wasn't part of the human species.

Her Opa had told her to look at the eyes and sure enough, the man trying to stalk her had gold eyes. Another dragon. Interesting.

Hara was curious now and watched the two dragons carefully. The other man, though tall like the others, didn't have the gold eyes so she guessed he was a human after all.

The three were arguing now. She wasn't sure what they were arguing over, but the human waved his hands and the two dragons went silent and glared at each other.

Into the silence, Hara said, "Well, Gideon, you are home and I have to go. Maybe we can talk another time."

Angel chirped a goodbye.

Hara turned to leave, but Gideon caught her arm and turned her to face him.

Gideon said, "Something to think about."

He surprised her by kissing her. A light brush of his lips over hers. It was very chaste and he didn't try to take it further. Gideon stroked Angel's head when she chirped for equal attention. She was flustered, but shook herself and left. She decided that if she said anything, she might just make a fool of yourself.

Hopefully, the dragon and his companion could distract Gideon so she could leave the city without him sneaking back.

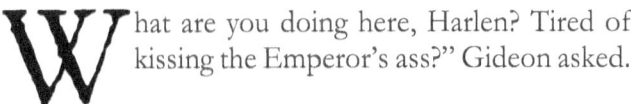

What are you doing here, Harlen? Tired of kissing the Emperor's ass?" Gideon asked.

85

The other man, the Empire agent, whom Gideon didn't know, huffed. "Can we leave the insults for another time? We came here because we are concerned about you."

Gideon glared at Harlen, then turned to the agent. "There is no need for concern. The Rosh Barkers have already tried and have failed in keeping me."

Harlen gasped. "What?"

He glared at the agent, who shrugged and said, "Our information is usually timelier than this."

Gideon shook his head. "It doesn't matter. I might seem like I can't look after myself, but I've been looking after myself since I was born. You two can get out of my home."

The Agent jumped at the look in Gideon's eyes. He obviously didn't deal with dragons very often.

Harlen wasn't intimidated. "It seems like you haven't been here for a while. I take it you have interests elsewhere."

Gideon growled. Knowing Harlen spoke about Hara. "Yes, and she is mine."

Harlen raised an eyebrow to show his own astonishment and Gideon added, "Your Emperor does not have to worry. I won't be joining his enemies. I'll bond with a human and that will no longer be a concern."

Harlen said in a soft voice, "You are not a burden, Gideon."

Gideon snorted. "That isn't what he said the last time we spoke. I am not in his collection and I never will abide by his rules. He has always worried I would join someone else's collection. He forgets we are all blood and, unlike you, I don't need to grovel to feel completed."

Harlen's face darkened, but he didn't argue with Gideon on that point. After a long moment, he said, "Keep yourself safe. The Rosh Barkers might take another chance at you."

Gideon nodded his head, acknowledging that Harlen cared. At least, that was honest. After all, they shared a mother. Though dragons didn't usually have their own flesh and blood in their collections the three of them had found each other and were as close to family as dragons could be. But he and Harlen had never gotten along although they had never been enemies either.

On their home planet Gideon had not had much status while his brothers had all held positions of power though not as high as they had wished. When they had come to earth they were forced to leave everything behind so there had been no ranks or status. Gideon with the part he had played in bringing everyone to earth rose in status. And yet he had never used that to gain anything. It had confused the other dragons. They had turned to his brothers who were more traditional when it came to dragon hierarchy. There had been chaos as those who wanted power greedily collected all they could to gain in social status.

Catherine had finally been the tipping point for his oldest brother. She had been a woman set up as a tribute to dragons. She had been taken by Erasmus his and Harlen's oldest brother. He liked her stories and her wit and during a raid by dragon hunters; she had been hurt and he had saved her. At the same moment, bonding with her.

She gave birth to William less than a year later. Erasmus being able to have children because of his collection shot to the top of the social ranking. He became the first Emperor of dragons on the planet. William himself had grown up to have the same ambition as his father and had conquered most of Europe. He had called himself an emperor as well, like his father. Erasmus made a treaty with his son and from then on he forced all the dragons to play nicely with the humans.

Since Gideon had never eaten humans and had a status that rivalled his brother, they had left him out of the treaty. Partly because they couldn't find him. He had been living amongst humans at that stage. Gideon had never been part of the Dragon Empire. And he wasn't going to start taking orders now.

Hara was startled when a young man approached her on the street. She didn't pause as he matched her pace.

He cleared his throat. "Miss. Miss, I hear you have work?"

He was young. Maybe only fifteen. She glanced at him. He was wringing his hands in nervousness.

Hara asked, "This is a big city. Surely you can get a job here."

He sighed. "Well, you see, I live in this neighbourhood with my Ma. But there is this guy. He wants me to steal for him. But I don't want to. If I stick around in the city, I might not have a choice, you see." He lowered his voice. "I've read about your grandfather. He was famous in his day. I want to work with someone who can help me be something more."

Hara glanced at him again. He was still keeping up with her, even though she was striding at a fast clip through the city streets. They were short on crew and she really couldn't be picky. He was probably a thief who got into trouble with his fence or something. She didn't think he was innocent.

Hara shrugged. "Come along. We'll see." She doubted that he knew about her work with her father. But probably hoped she would introduce him to her grandfather. It was almost pleasant to be recognized for that part of the family instead of the cons she had done when she was younger.

They were fast approaching the Blazing Blunderbuss. The airship really was a beauty. Even with the scar down the side where the cannon ball had just grazed it. It was cosmetic so they had left it when they had completed the other repairs. She actually thought it made her prettier. The Blazing Blunderbuss has been a survivor, just like she was.

Hara hated Gideon at that moment as he was right. She liked the idea of being captain of her own ship. The Blazing Blunderbuss was quickly becoming her home. But she admitted she would miss Gideon. He was quirky and interesting and he had saved her life at least once.

Alice greeted them as they approached the ship. She was more bubbly than usual.

Alice skipped along beside her after Hara and the boy had climbed up the ladder. Alice said, "I got us a cargo, captain. It's small but they were willing to pay a lot for it."

Hara raised an eyebrow at Alice. "That sounds a little too good to be true. Tell me the details."

Alice finally noticed the boy who was following her and asked, "Who is that?"

Hara glanced at the boy and realised she had hired the boy without even knowing his name. The boy stuttered for a moment, then flushed and finally said, "I'm Liam. I... I... I'm going to be..."

Hara came to his rescue as he clearly didn't know how to talk to girls his own age. "Alice, this is our new midshipman. Henry will appreciate getting out of the boiler room more often and the food should improve with his mood."

Alice grinned. "He actually made soufflé today since he didn't have to stoke the boiler. The cargo is already loaded. We can go whenever you want."

Hara had no reason to stick around so she said, "Right away. Gideon had some visitors when I took him home. I think they might distract him long enough for us to get away."

Alice blinked in confusion. "Gideon wanted to stay on the ship? I thought this whole trip was to get him home."

Hara said, "He wants more than a trip on the airship, Alice."

The boy snickered.

Alice frowned as she thought this over and said when she finally figured out what she meant. "But what do you feel about it?"

Hara sighed at the woman's perception. "I'll be nice this time Alice as you don't know any better, but the truth is that it isn't any of your business."

Alice flushed and quickly said, "Sorry, Captain. You're completely right. It is none of my business. Let me settle in the boy in the boiler room and I can report back to you about the cargo."

Since it was already loaded, she would take it even if it was too good to be true. There would certainly be strings attached. Alice was a kind soul. She would learn soon enough that some things weren't to be trusted and a good deal was one of those.

The boy leaned over the railing as they walked through the cargo area towards the bridge. "Man, this is high up."

Alice chuckled. "You haven't seen anything yet. We are low for docking. This beautiful beast can go a lot higher."

Hara said, "I hope you aren't afraid of heights."

Henry yelled from further in the ship, "Hurry up, dinner is almost ready."

Hara said, "It might have to wait a short while. I want to head out first." She turned to Alice and asked, "So, where are we going, Alice?"

Alice checked a piece of paper with the details of the delivery. "Kerak."

Hara closed her eyes and tilted her head back. Her lips moved in a silent prayer.

Henry groaned and Alice asked, "What?"

Hara opened her eyes and said, "It isn't a very pleasant place to go. Not to worry. We'll be there in under a week and during that time I think I'll show you how to read the smugglers' code. We can avoid this in the future." The string attached to this cargo wasn't ideal but it wasn't too bad.

Kerak was a raider's town. They had been the home to killers and assassins since William conquered most of Europe and forced their element to hide at the edges of the empire. Kerak in those days had been further away from the border than it was today. The violent elements there hadn't got any tamer as so-called civilisation got closer. It would be an interesting trip, but she had been there before and had survived.

Hara rolled out one map. She said, "These are in code. So you need to know the code before you can understand it. Here is the symbol for the ports. Next to it shows what facilities they have."

Hara pulled a piece of paper closer and drew the symbols she was talking about and put translations beside them. "These ports can repair and deal with most issues in engineering. These here show where you can get guns."

She looked at Alice significantly. "You want to avoid any of these towns. To get the guns, you have to run on the black market. There is no law in these towns."

Alice blushed. "Is Kerak one of those towns?"

Hara didn't want to hurt the girl, but she needed to know if she was going to stay on the ship. "Yes. Here is Kerak."

The port was in the Middle East. In the area still under dispute after the last move by the empire over a hundred years before. There was a delicate peace of sorts, but it could easily turn to full out war. The men there tended to be as rough as the area they lived in as they were squeezed by the empire and the rest of civilisation in the rest of the middle east. They had little time or patience with the criminal element.

Alice asked shyly. "Is it really dangerous?"

Again Hara didn't hold back. "Yes. So when we go there, no one is leaving the ship except those going with me. But Alice, that isn't the issue. The deal sounded great? Well, there was a reason. Next time, take someone else with you. They can help you see the tricks as you learn."

Alice sniffed. "Maybe I shouldn't make any more deals."

Hara shook her head. "Don't be like that, Alice. You'll learn." Besides, the last time Hara had gone looking for the cargo, she couldn't get anyone to talk to her. Alice must have some special charm to get men to talk business with her. It would be better to teach her how to look for tricks than trying to get Hara to learn how to be personable. Which at the moment looked like a miracle if it happened. Alice learning was merely a matter of time.

The wind caressed his skin. Gideon pumped his wings and thought he really should do this more often. He had spent the last few decades playing with numbers in various universities around the Empire. He had forgotten what it was like to fly over the plains. The feel of the air and space around him. He had waited for it to get dark before he had set off as he hated scaring the populous with his form.

He liked night flying the best. The sense of space was infinite. It seemed he was flying through space itself. The only thing which compared to this feeling was when he was with Hara. The way she thought and her wit thrilled him like dropping from a height and watching the ground rush towards him.

Gideon flipped a loop in the air as he flew. He wasn't too far from the Blazing Blunderbuss and he was considering how angry Hara was going to be. She would see her trip to the city as pointless. Her eyes would probably spark. She also wouldn't be shocked. She was far from stupid and she would know he had wings and he would follow her. She would have picked her destination at the last minute to give him the slip. But he could smell her on the air. It wouldn't matter which way she went, he would be able to follow her.

Gideon saw the ship in the distance. It had a few running lights lit as it moved through the air. Grinning, he approached cautiously. He didn't grab onto the ship as he usually did when he was in dragon form. Instead, he placed himself above the ship and changed to human form.

Gideon dropped onto the envelope holding the gasses, which kept the ship afloat. He slid down the side and caught one of the ropes and brought himself to a stop. He hung there for a moment, grinning.

It didn't take long for Gideon to make his way onto the deck and to sneak further into the ship.

Instead of going to his room, he made his way to the stateroom. It was time to move things forward a bit more. Especially because Hara had returned the kiss in his apartment. She had been timid, but there had been heat there. She felt it like he did. He could have pushed it then if only there hadn't been company. But he would be patient. He had the time after all.

He knew with any other woman this would be stalking but Hara was different. He had worried about that enough that he had left the bracelets in her room the night before they had arrived in the city. If she had truly wanted him to stay in the city she would have made him wear the bracelets. Instead, he had found the bracelets back on his bed this morning with a note that said he needed to forget her as she was trouble. He knew the message was there. That it would be his choice to follow her or not but that he would have to face whatever trouble she thought she would bring. Compared to his own issues her trouble couldn't be as troublesome.

When he got to her stateroom, the only one there was the metal flying creature. The clockwork dragon slept in a small hollow on the bed. He wrinkled his nose at the creature. It lifted its head and trilled at him with a question.

Gideon crouched down so he was close to the creature. He would not call it a dragon. He narrowed his eyes. "Let us get this clear. Hara is going to be my queen. You make her happy so you will remain in her life, but you will not hinder me."

The creature chirped and it must have understood somewhat as it uncurled itself and moved it somewhere else to sleep.

Eyeing the bed, Gideon grinned. Sass had always suited him before. He wasn't about to stop. Hara was going to be mad with him anyway. He might as well make it interesting.

———————————

Hara was exhausted. They hadn't been able to afford more people to help them load the supplies so she had pitched in with the others earlier in the evening. They had done a good job to get it all on board but only Henry had known how to load cargo and he had been cooking. It meant moving everything around before they could get any real height.

An airship which wasn't loaded right could tip in the stronger breezes higher up in the atmosphere. They had all pitched in to move things quickly. But it meant her muscles now ached.

Hara didn't turn up the light in her cabin. She would just fall on the bed and sleep. She was that exhausted. Henry had served cheese and crackers for a late supper, but she didn't complain. She had been too tired to even eat. Alice was taking the night watch. She was feeling a bit guilty for taking the cargo in the first place.

Hara regretted making her feel guilty for picking a dangerous cargo. She was young. This wouldn't be her last mistake and Hara certainly had made her own mistakes. She would talk with the girl in the morning. At least the girl had got them a cargo.

Hara stripped off her leathers and ran a hand through her loosened hair. She sat on the edge of her bed, but it wasn't for long. She jumped to her feet when she sat on something which shouldn't be there.

Gideon grunted and rolled over. "Hey, sweetheart."

Hara went to the light and turned it up so she could see Gideon sleeping in her bed.

She growled. "Gideon!"

She had known that he could find them but she had hoped it would take him at least a day to catch up with them. After all he hadn't known what direction they had been heading.

He sat up in bed and she was shocked to see he didn't have a shirt on. She turned because she didn't want to see what he wasn't wearing as he sat up. She could feel a blush on her cheeks. She was mad at herself as he didn't have anything she hadn't seen before. She had been disguised as a boy for most of her life. And men and boys didn't try to hide from other boys.

Hara said, "Put some clothes on, Gideon." She could hear the rustle of cloth but determinedly stared at the wall.

He asked, "Are you sure you don't want a peek?"

She rolled her eyes and said firmly, "I'm not going to speak to you while you are half dressed."

Gideon said, "Are you sure you are going to speak? I was so sure you would yell. I was looking forward to a heated argument. You are very pretty when you argue."

She spun to glare at him. Gideon grinned at her as he said, "Wow, I really did think that comment would get you riled up. Are you going to yell at me?"

He had pants on but he still hadn't put on a shirt. She blushed and turned away again. He was very well formed for a mathematician. Although she wondered if that was just a trick dragon could do to make them look appealing in their human form.

Gideon said, "You can turn around now. I have clothes on. Though I have to say it would have been a much more interesting conversation if I was naked."

When she turned around, he was sitting on her bed, dressed at least.

Hara ran a hand through her hair. "What are you doing here?"

He leant back on the bed. "I told you. I want you to be part of my collection."

Hara frowned. "No matter how you explain being in your collection is not slavery, I still can't stop the shiver which goes down my spine every time you say it."

Gideon cocked his head to the side and studied her for a long moment. He shifted so he was further on the bed and patted the blankets next to him. "Sit, we can talk."

Hara contemplated for a moment yelling at him and throwing him literally overboard. In the end, she thought she would be grown up about it and sit on the bed with him and talk it out. She told herself it had nothing to do with the fact that Gideon was good looking and annoying as he was, she was happy he was back.

"I'm not keen on being in your collection," Hara said as she took a seat. Tucking her knees up under her chin.

He asked casually. "Is it just me or something else?"

Hara shook her head. There were so many things wrong with that question, she wasn't sure where to start. "My dad is a con artist. He made me realise you can't trust anyone. Mostly men. I don't want to belong to anyone. My father always used me and I escaped. I don't want to go back to that. Do you understand?"

Gideon watched her for a long while. "All I ask is for the chance to prove to you I am not like your father."

Hara looked at him with a critical eye. "And what does that entail?"

Gideon grinned. "Sticking around."

She rolled her eyes. She flopped back onto the bed and said with a sigh, "Fine, you can stay, but that doesn't mean anything alright."

He grinned. "I'm alright with that." He pulled his legs up and propped his head on the top of them. "It might seem scary to keep me around but I understand."

She shook her head. She sat on the bed next to him. "You say that now but you don't know my past."

He shrugged. "That is alright as well. One day you will share with me." He reached out and laid his hand lightly on her hand. "I have a crazy family as well."

She snorted at the idea.

"No, I'm serious. My oldest brother is super controlling. I had to go years not even speaking to any of them just to find a space that was my own. Whenever I see my other brother it reminds me what will happen to me if I ever let my guard down and let him control me."

She was quiet for a long moment. "I didn't realise dragons had family dramas."

He chuckled. "We are a lot more volatile than humans. So of course there is more drama."

She gave him a glance. "Is that supposed to make me want to keep you around?" he shifted off the bed and stood up.

"Yes, it means I'll make your life interesting."

His hand was on the door when he turned around. "About the kiss."

She waved him off. She didn't want to talk about it. But he went on anyway. "You should have the next move." She frowned at him and he added, "I'm not going to chase you Hara because no one deserves to be hounded. So I'll wait. You can kiss me next."

She let out a sigh. There weren't any words for what she felt but she appreciated that he had put into words what their relationship would be. She waved him away and he flashed her a smile before leaving.

Kerak was a sprawling town. It really could have been classed as a city if it had bothered to go through the paperwork to be classified as such. Landing in the port had been a simple affair, attesting to need necessitating efficiency.

There were a couple of roughs running the port but they were gruff yet fair. She knew if they broke any of the rules, they wouldn't be so fair then. She had Gideon and Henry to carry the trunk. It was light, but awkward.

Hara had looked inside, even though there was a very complicated lock on it. She had worried it was drugs and if that had been the case. She would have taken it back to its owner and told them to go shove it. She was amused when she found it was filled with spices. Rare and exotic and really difficult to acquire spices, but only innocuous spices. She was pretty sure they were stolen, but then so was her ship. She really couldn't be all high and mighty and moral when it came to stealing.

Hara led the way with the notes Alice had taken from the client. She knew Kerak vaguely. She and her father had hidden out in one of the taverns here. Her father had been running away from an Empire noble whom he had conned into buying a mine which didn't exist.

Seeing the place now that she was older, Hara was shocked her father had brought a child here. The streets had women of ill repute on every corner. The men swore and cursed loudly. Hara thought her father probably was oblivious to the behaviour of the residents of Kerak. She certainly had been as a child.

Leaning against a plastered building that had seen better days was someone watching them. They were half in the shadows of the building next to it. He looked familiar, but she had stayed here for a while and it might be someone she had known from her past. She dismissed him easily.

The tavern where they were to meet the clients was at the end of the street. A quick signal to the inn

101

keeper and they were led to a private room at the back. Gideon put the trunk down and settled on top of it.

Hara said to Henry, "Head back and grab some supplies. We should be along shortly."

She said the last a bit louder because the door was open already and the people they were supposed to meet had arrived. Henry ducked past the clients as they entered and returned to the airship.

Their clients were the typical over muscled men she had expected to be picking up stolen goods. She stood next to Gideon, who was inspecting his nails in an overly casual way. He would not seem like the most dangerous person in the room.

One of her clients motioned to the trunk with his head and asked, "Is that what we are here for?"

Hara placed her hands on her hips. "That depends if you brought the money."

The leader didn't answer. He motioned for his men to move forward. She didn't wait. She pulled out her gun and pointed it at him.

Gideon said, "Wow, that escalated fast. I really did think there would be some posturing, a few insults maybe."

The other men pulled out their weapons and pointed them at the two of them. The tension was thick as people pointed guns at each other. The clients couldn't decide if she was the dangerous one or Gideon and kept changing their target. Hara didn't move and her aim was directed at the leader.

Hara said, "We can all leave here without holes in our pretty flesh if you can provide us with what we are due."

The leader said, "I could just kill you. And take what we want." He wasn't a very bright smuggler if he thought this was the way to do business. If he continued this way, it would be a matter of time before he was adorned with extra iron himself.

Hara motioned with her gun to indicate her gun was aimed at him as she said, "But I would shoot you first. Not anyone else. Just you. Now, are you going to give the order for me to be shot and for you to die?"

There was a tense silence, then the leader motioned to one of his men. They placed a small purse on the ground.

Hara asked Gideon. "How much is there?" He didn't even leave his seat on top of the trunk as he said, "Fifty gold coins. All in brass and copper and one ceramic penny. Do they still use ceramic pennies here? How archaic."

Hara ignored his extraneous comments. The amount was exactly what they had been promised. She didn't question how he could know how much money there was. Dragons had their own tricks.

Hara said, "Pick it up, Gideon. We are leaving."

Gideon hopped off the trunk and picked up the purse. He tucked it away and came to stand behind her.

He asked, "Are you going to shoot him?"

"Not now. But?" She raised an eyebrow. The leader motioned to his men and they put down their guns. She did as well. She tipped her head to the man. "Enjoy your loot. Come along Gideon."

They stepped out of the room.

A man leaning against the wall outside said, "I was just about to come in and rescue you, baby girl."

Hara frowned at the man, then realised who he was. "Talen?"

This was who she had seen outside and thought familiar. He had been an ex-convict who had worked with her father. He was mostly a thief who broke into houses to find out things about people. He used to steal things, but he said that was too easy, so he had gone into stealing information instead.

Talen moved away from the wall and approached her. He gave her a hug and kissed her cheek. She pulled away when she heard Gideon growled behind her. He was a dragon after all and he might do something stupid like attack her old friend.

Hara asked, "What are you doing here, Talen?"

Talen shrugged. "Getting stuck in this two-bit town. I saw you had a ship and I thought I could bum a ride out of this place. Well, at least to a place where people aren't trying to kill me."

She shook her head slightly, not at all surprised someone was trying to kill him. "Talen, I don't think I can find a town this side of the world where there is no one trying to kill you."

Talen rolled his eyes at her humour. "Ha ha. Well, is there space for a slightly redeemed thief?"

Hara grinned. "Definitely, but you might need to man the guns if we ever get in trouble. And the rest of the crew will be your friends for life if you take a stint stoking the fires in the engine room."

Gideon huffed. "Do we have to bring him along? You already got that clockwork nonsense." She had left Angel back on the ship. Though she had to bribe the creature with a glass bauble.

She smiled when she turned to Gideon and asked, "Jealous." Of Talen or Angel, she didn't particularly care which.

Gideon huffed again. "Of course I am."

Hara laughed outright at that. Talen raised an eyebrow and asked, "Is this your man?"

"He certainly wants to be but we are still negotiating. Have you got all your gear, Talen? I think we should leave this town as soon as possible before those men decide they want their money back."

Gideon came to walk next to her. He said in a hissed whisper, "Do you trust him? At least the clockwork monster is harmless."

"Yes, surprisingly. Certainly more than the rest of the crew. You do know they are all strangers. Don't worry, Gideon, jealousy is a nasty emotion. You'll get used to it. Just breathe out slowly and it will go away." She liked that Gideon was jealous. It was a very human emotion.

———————

They were out of Kerak without any incident. Alice had stopped apologising so life was good. Talen had headed to his room with a saunter. Gideon approached her. He had been sulking over dinner as she and Talen had reminisced over past pranks.

Talen had been careful not to mention anything about her father so he must have heard of what her father had done to her. Leaving her to serve prison time.

Gideon leant on the railing next to her. Angel sat on the railing and clung on with her small claws as the wind buffeted her. She remained there with the two of them for a long while. Eventually, she turned to him. "I'm not going to sleep with Talen. He is like an older brother."

Gideon turned to her, his eyes warm. "I don't like this feeling." He reached out and stroked one of Angel's wings. She turned her head to trill at him. Hara caught his hand and tugged him closer. He stood in front of her. She studied him. He was taller than her and he was in a serious need of a good haircut.

Hara reached up and moved his hair away from his face. "You didn't eat him, though. No more than you crushed Angel."

Gideon shook his head. "I don't eat humans. Never did. The others didn't like that I was so queasy about taking lives and that I lived away from them." That was curious, she thought.

Hara asked, "Is that why you got into an argument with that dragon in your house?"

Gideon nodded. "The Emperor of the dragons believes we are all in his collection. I am not in his collection. He cannot order me around."

"So, do you think you'll be able to order me around if I'm in your collection?"

Hara was starting to understand this collection thing. There were good things about it and other things which rankled with her.

Gideon shrugged non-committedly and she dug a little deeper. "Would I have to follow any of your orders?"

He wrinkled his nose and eventually said, "I don't like following orders so I would not expect orders to be followed. But I can't guarantee I won't try to order you around."

She smiled at him. This collection thing didn't sound as bad as she thought. She went up on her toes and kissed him. Much like the kiss he had given her in his house. Lightly and on the lips.

Hara stepped back and patted his chest. "We'll see."

She gathered up Angel and left him there. She wasn't sure why she said that as she still had no intention of being his collection.

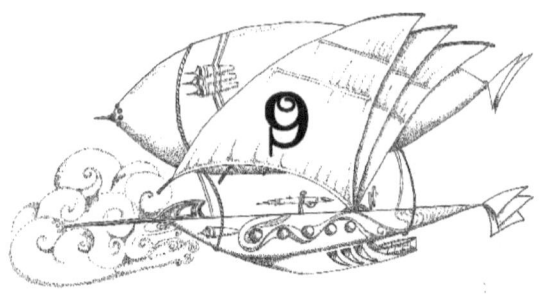

Gideon moved through the narrow corridors of the airship. Kale was coming towards him. It was late and it was strange to have anyone but those on watch to be wandering around. Gideon stopped the man by stepping in front of him.

Kale huffed. "Hey, man. What's up?"

Gideon frowned at the tone which accompanied the words as they didn't match. Gideon tilted his head as he studied the man.

Kale said, "Henry's hot cakes this evening aren't sitting right by me." There was just a touch of disgust to his tone.

Gideon tilted his head the other way. "You will not harm anyone on this ship." It wasn't a threat but Gideon's tone was very serious.

Kale frowned. "Hey, where did that come from? I'm here to make sure nothing goes wrong. That is what muscle is for." That sounded like the truth.

Gideon nodded sharply. "Just make sure that stays true, Kale. Wait until Henry makes soufflé that will sit right."

He flashed Kale a grin. The man didn't know how to take the sudden change in Gideon's mood. He gave a half-hearted chuckle and squeezed past Gideon.

Gideon might have followed the man to see what he really was up to but he had better things to do.

———————————

Hara's hair was loose over the pillow. Hands moved through her hair. Lips brushed over her collarbone. She arched into the touch. She groaned. Flesh moved against flesh. She had dreams like this before. She settled in to enjoy it.

She ran her hands over his shoulders and then up into his hair. The hair was longer than she was used to in these dreams. About as long as Gideon's hair. The man in her arms was suddenly very much Gideon.

Hara hesitated for a moment, then thought it was just a dream and where was the harm in that? But just as she was getting into it, she was rudely woken with a hand over her mouth.

Cold steel pressed to her cheek. A voice harshly said into the darkness. "Don't make a move, Captain."

It was Kale. Darn. She had thought her policy of taking on everyone might bite her in the arse. It might get more interesting when Kale tried to wake up Gideon though.

Kale swore as Angel attacked him. He let Hara go to fling Angel off him and threw her small body against the wall. There was a crunch and she went limp. Hara used the opportunity to reach for her tool belt on the bedside table. Her legs tangled in her blankets and her fingers barely brushed the belt when Kale shoved her face first into her bedding. He grunted with pain as he moved.

Kale stood her up. She struggled in his grasp. "At least let me put on some clothes."

He eyed her in her nightgown. He grabbed her dirty clothes, which were over a chair, and threw them at her. He also pulled out a gun and pointed it at her. "No funny business."

She dressed quickly. As Hara was shoved out of the room, she saw out of the corner of her eye that Angel had moved a little. Relief rushed through.

Hara was frog marched onto the bridge. She groaned when she saw Gideon was already tied up with the others. So much for Gideon showing his true self and putting an end to this farce. They were all sitting on the ground under the window in the front of the bridge. Murphy looked angry and Alice scared. Gideon on the other hand looked curious. When he caught her eye he mouthed, "Are you alright?" She nodded her head.

Hara had been the last to be rounded up. She was tied up and forced down next to the others.

She whispered to Gideon, "How did they get you?"

He leaned over and said just as quietly said, "Those bracelets. I told you they make things sticky."

So much for hoping Gideon would save them once again.

Hara glared at Kale as he turned the ship from their course. Gideon had told her he didn't think the Rosh Barkers knew he was a dragon, but why then would they keep using the bands if they didn't know he was a dragon? She sat with her knees tucked up to her chest.

She asked after a while. "What does the Rosh Barkers want with us?"

Kale kept his eyes on the map and the wheel as he answered, "Not you, but the mathematician."

He didn't question that she had assumed it was the Rosh Barkers who wanted Gideon. Confirming that Gideon wasn't so unlucky to have two groups chasing after him.

Gideon asked, "For what? Because I have to admit I'm good with numbers and stuff but really, I'm not good for much. Just ask Hara. She will tell you I'm pretty much useless."

Hara snorted. "He doesn't even take his turn in the engine room. And he can't cook."

There was a grunt from one of the men, but Hara didn't turn to them to see who it was. She would have guessed Henry.

Kale said blandly, "You'll be told when you get there."

Gideon wasn't ready to leave it alone, though. "Won't it be better if I have more time to think of it? I mean, maths is about thinking."

Kale hesitated and Hara wondered if he would answer at all.

Then Kale said, "There is a machine which was made before the Empire. It was never completed. We have finished making it, but we now need help calibrating it so it can be used."

Interesting, Hara thought. A machine made before the Empire would mean it was a weapon to take down dragons. Dragons had been the shadow who made everyone shiver in the past when they flew over. Raining death and destruction, they were the only thing people feared enough to concentrate enough to make a sophisticated weapon for. Especially if

111

finishing it had been no longer a priority when the dragons made the treaty.

Why would the Rosh barkers want a weapon to kill dragons? Now if it was the Rosh government, she could understand. The Empire was looking towards Rosh. With a weapon to use against dragons, they would be able to neutralise a large part of the Empire's force if they ever attacked.

The braclets! She glanced at Gideon. Those bracelets would have been difficult to acquire. But not for an entity as large and powerful as the Rosh government. Now if they tricked a group like the Rosh barkers into making a weapon to use on the dragons, they could test it without having to worry about retaliation against Rosh itself.

Instead of working against the government, the Rosh Barkers were being used by them. Poor bastards.

Liam gasped and she looked to see where he was staring. It was Angel. She crawled along the wall. She was dragging one of her wings, but otherwise looked whole. It wouldn't be hard to fix that. Hara called to Angel and she scurried across to her and whimpered as the small creature cuddled up to her.

Kale huffed, still concentrating on flying the ship. "I thought that thing was destroyed." He pulled his gun out but he wasn't fast enough. Angel hid behind Hara. Kale wrinkled his nose and put his gun away.

Interesting that Kale didn't want to kill them. Obviously, he was planning to use her as leverage against Gideon. But that wasn't wise.

G ideon was shoved forward and he glared at Kale. Nikolai was standing before them and Gideon turned to the leader. Kale was a bastard, but he didn't really have any power in this situation.

Gideon flicked his head so his hair was out of his face. "Ah, Nikolai, old pal. You have really bad timing. I'm courting a lady and you have really put a kink in my plans of amore."

Nikolai snarled silently, wrinkling up his nose. "Professor, your jovial nature seems very misplaced. If you try to escape again, I'll kill your crew. Including your lady friend."

Gideon waved off the threat with his tied hands. "Oh, they aren't my crew. They are Hara's. I'm not sure why she keeps picking up strays, but it seems to make her happy…" Gideon wanted to rip Nikolai apart for the threat to Hara, but that wouldn't be very productive at this point while Gideon didn't have access to the teeth and claw which would do the most damage. He would let the revolutionary underestimate him.

Nikolai cut him off. "Enough Professor. We are willing to let you live and your strays, as you call them, if you will fix something for us."

Hara had hinted to him before they had arrived that the thing needing fixing was meant to kill dragons. Gideon was sure of it. There weren't many mathematicians who could calibrate a weapon to shoot something out of the sky. None of them could predict a dragon's movements enough to make it accurate enough to be a danger to any dragon. But with him, that was a different thing. The ones who had captured him for the Rosh Barkers had probably assumed because he had no liking for the Empire rules, he hated the Empire.

Gideon motioned with his tied hands to indicate he knew about the weapon. "Yes, your lackey here mentioned something along those lines. So what is this thing you want me to fix? I would appreciate if we could hurry this along so I can get to back to my lady."

Nikolai didn't seem pleased Kale had been sharing secrets. "That is not important. You just need to fix it."

Gideon would enjoy annoying the Rosh Barkers for the threat they were to Hara. "Oh, I disagree. If it is a machine to make chopped liver, then the equations are very different from saying something which flies through the air. So I do need to know what the machine does."

There was a long silence from everyone in the room. Nikolai liked his men to crowd around him, it seemed. As there were twice as many men this time as there had been when they had opened his crate in the inn after the first time they had kidnapped him.

Nikolai eventually said, "It is a machine which shoots bolts of steel into the sky. We have tried it and it shoots, but with no accuracy. We need you to fix this."

Gideon shrugged. "No problem. I might need Hara's help. She is a brilliant engineer as well as the Captain. I'm good with numbers, but just look at these hands. Do they look like they have done a day of work in my life? Heaven forbid, I might mess up my manicure." Gideon wriggled his fingers in Nikolai's face. Not that he had a manicure but he

114

knew the Roshian wouldn't know that. He was playing a part and hoped it would make the man less likely to watch him closely.

Nikolai narrowed his eyes, but ignored his rant and instead said, "Your friends will be staying here on the ship. As a guarantee for your good behaviour. You will have to fix it on your own. Even if it means breaking a nail."

Gideon knew all their lives were measured in hours instead of years as long as that machine was working. For both dragons and the Rosh Barkers. While it existed the dragons would stop at nothing to destroy it and they wouldn't care who was in the way either.

He would have to do something to stall. He would know when he saw the machine. It would have been easier with Hara. She would have been able to put something together with a piece of string and a rubber band which would take down all these men. Ah well, he would have to come up with something. Hopefully, it wasn't a terrible idea.

Gideon asked, "Why do you need a weapon like this, anyway? You guys look like strong men." He eyed up one of the men standing next to Nikolai. The man looked like he had more muscles than brains. When the man glared at Gideon, he blew him a kiss. The Rosh barker frowned in confusion.

Nikolai spat on the ground. "We are staring down the barrel of the Empire guns and you ask why we would need a weapon. We do not wish to be the next piece of land to be added to the empire. We will not be trodden down in the dust."

Nikolai went on for a while berating the empire and how they, the last bastion of the Roshian people, would fight to their dying breath. The typical rhetoric of revolutionaries and none of it really meant anything. Gideon wished he had one of those machines which could record sound and show these people what was really coming out of their mouths but he doubted it would make any difference.

All he could do was stall until he found a way to escape. Hopefully a way which destroyed the weapon at the same time. Oh, and of course free Hara. If she hadn't managed to come and swoop him off his feet in the meantime. He didn't want to bet who did the rescuing first as he wasn't sure he would win. He grinned at the thought of Hara rescuing him, but Nikolai thought it was for something he had said.

Nikolai grunted. "Good. Then you will fix the machine for us."

Gideon blinked in confusion. Nikolai didn't seem to notice and motioned for all of them to leave the airship.

Hara felt Angel behind her. She scratched at Hara's wrists and she was about to shoo the small clockwork dragon away. Angel then started gnawing on her ropes, which bound her hands behind her.

Hara shifted forward a little to give Angel more room. Her timing was off as Kale returned and eyed her suspiciously.

Liam asked softly, "What do you think they will do to us?" Kale glanced at the boy and then went to the door, where another guard waited.

Hara said, "Once they get what they want, they will kill us and drop our bodies in a place where we will never be found."

Murphy grunted. "If we are lucky and they don't have any other need for us." He turned his head and eyed Liam and continued, "You are a pretty boy. I wonder what kind of price you will get on the slave market."

Liam went white and Alice hissed at Murphy. "You don't have to scare the boy. We all know what we would be in for if we were sold as slaves." That might be true for Alice, who had an inkling of what men wanted from her. Liam probably knew as well what someone would want from him as well.

Talen said, "It won't come to that."

Murphy sneered. "Oh, so you reckon you can escape?"

Hara hissed. "Leave it alone, guys. We won't be sold as slaves and we aren't going to be killed. I promise you that."

Angel finished chewing through her ropes, but Hara didn't move. Angel hesitated, then must have realised what Hara wanted and moved out from behind her and moved on to the others.

<hr />

Gideon had managed to fix the weapon in a few minutes. The equations to hit what the weapon was aimed for had been simple and all it had needed to be done was the tightening of some things and making sure the ring used to aim was in the right spot.

Gideon had that in his hand now as he waved it around and nattered. He didn't know how long it would take for Hara to come to him, but he had to stall until then. He had already figured out what to do

117

with the weapon before he left to make sure the weapon wouldn't harm anyone.

The winch was powered by a steam engine and it wouldn't take much to make the whole contraption over heat and blow itself up. Nikolai was watching him personally. He had actually sent away his entourage.

Gideon tapped the weapon with the aiming tool and said conversationally while Nikolai winced at his cavalier nature. "So this is to kill dragons. What have dragons done to you, by the way? I mean recently. I know they used to chomp on people and eat them. They haven't done that in hundreds of years."

Nikolai grunted. "They are the tool of the Empire and the Empire wants to chew us up. That is just as bad."

Gideon leant on the arm of the large crossbow like thing. "True. You'd think the government would agree with you. Surely it would be easier to fight this war with the government on your side."

Nikolai snorted. "They are fools. They coddle up to the Empire in an attempt to convince them not to attack. It is a fool's task. You can't negotiate with a beast."

Gideon lifted his hand and motioned to the wrists and asked, "Where did you get these?"

Nikolai growled. He was obviously tired of the talking. He pulled out a gun and pointed it at Gideon. "Fix it or die, professor."

Gideon lifted his hands to show he was defenceless and said, "Easy, easy. I'm delicate, you know. I faint at the sight of blood. Especially my own."

Nikolai huffed, but put down his gun and Gideon placed the aiming ring where it was supposed to be. As he worked, Nikolai said, "The wrist guards are to make sure you don't go nowhere."

Gideon knew that, but he was curious what Nikolai and the Rosh Barkers thought. Still fiddling with the ring, he asked without looking at Nikolai. "How does that work?"

He could see out of the corner of his eye that Nikolai shrugged. "Magic I suppose. A bit like the magic the dragon hunters have. I'm just not sure how it works for you. But the people said it was the only way to make you stayed in one place. And as you can see, it has worked. I think you might have some dragon hunter blood in you and that is why it works."

He wasn't wrong there, but it wasn't quite right either. The dragon hunters were Romani. Moving from area to area hunting dragons. They were almost completely wiped out by both humans and dragons since the treaty was signed. They were the only ones not safe under that contract.

Gideon had known a few in his day and the hunting of them had only made the dragon hunters irrational and more dangerous. Their magic was completely their own and had nothing to do with the dragons.

They had kept them on the Blazing blunderbuss. Hara's leg had gone to sleep sometime before so she was trying to get it past the pins and needles stage by stretching it out and banging her heel on the floor to encourage the blood to flow a little quicker.

One of the Rosh barkers yelled, "Stop that!"

Hara glared at the revolutionary. "What do you want me to do? Sitting on the ground is not the most comfortable thing. My leg and left butt cheek have gone to sleep."

Alice snorted. Hara glanced at her. She would have thought the girl would have been scared by the sudden violence, but the girl actually looked energised. This was one Pandora's box Hara had not expected to open.

Kale entered and the jovial nature disappeared. He dismissed the other guard and set himself to watch them.

Alice said in a whisper, "I never liked that guy. Sorry Henry. Even if he did save your life. He tried to hit on me and wasn't happy when I turned him down."

Hara shook her head. "It was my fault I hired the bastard. But I started this, you know, by taking Gideon from the Rosh Barkers in the first place."

"Yeah, it is your fault. And here I am, tied up like a pig set to be slaughtered," Murphy complained.

Hara turned to look at the gunner. "That is only because they took you so easily and they have your weapons."

"Yeah, they do and that rubs me the wrong way." Murphy grumbled softly.

Talen laughed. "Oh, you poor thing."

Everyone snorted at the sarcastic tone. "Don't try to help Talen. You just have to ignore him. I know the rest of us do," Henry added.

They laughed. Kale glared at them, but didn't try to shut them up.

Talen said out of the blue, "In three days I've become the two." That was an odd phrase. It hit her fast what was happening so when he said, "But no problem I knew on day One."

The two of them burst to their feet. Talen dived for a weapon while she went for Kale. He was shocked by the sudden movement. He tried to bring his gun up, but in his rush, he got tangled in the holster.

Hara slammed her palm into his face. He pulled back, reducing the effectiveness of the blow. She pushed forward and threw her elbow forward, hoping to hit him when he moved forward again.

Kale tried to punch her but she moved her arm to block the blow. He was surprised enough by her move that she was able to hit him squarely in his jaw with her other hand. His eyes rolled up in his head and he crumpled.

Talen came up to her side and she stepped around Kale. "I'm going for Gideon."

She could trust Talen to take care of the others now that Talen was armed. She didn't slow down as she dashed through the narrow corridors of the ship. Besides, Angel had freed the others as well and they were quickly moving to take the ship back.

She grabbed her glider and headed for the side of the ship, away from the ladder. She hoped she could get to the ground without the Rosh Barkers knowing. She strapped on her glider. She stopped for a moment as Angel hopped up on the railing.

Hara asked, "You want to come along?" Angel trilled. She had certainly been a help before. Hara offered an arm and Angel slithered up. She looked down and glad to see that the ship was moored higher than usual. She would need the height. Together, they then jumped off the side of the Blazing Blunderbuss.

Hara snapped open her wings and hoped to go unseen. The landing was rough, but she was down. She looked over her shoulder to see if anyone had seen her. Angel clicked her teeth together but didn't make any more noise. The guards were playing cards and laughing over something. Oblivious to her escape so they wouldn't have heard her anyway. Or their landing. Angel tightened her claws on her shoulder, but kept silent.

The Rosh Barkers probably thought they were safe because they were in the heart of their own territory in a hamlet which was filled with Rosh Barkers. She snapped her glider back into its case and ducked behind some buildings. Angel clicked her metal tongue at the whole thing.

Hara had no idea where they had taken Gideon, but if they had a weapon which could take down a dragon, it would have to be massive. This small hamlet really didn't have many buildings which could accommodate a large weapon.

She headed towards the large barn set to the side of the hamlet. She had seen a clear view of half the hamlet when she had come over the edge of the Blazing Blunderbuss. The barn had been the largest building she had seen. If Gideon and the weapon were in the other direction, it would make things difficult as she doubted she could stay undetected for that long.

There were plenty of Rosh Barkers wandering around so Hara moved slowly from cover to cover. She hoped they didn't discover the others were all free until much later. An explosion behind her made her duck to avoid any shrapnel. That was one of the Blazing Blunderbuss' guns. Angel trilled in concern and Hara reached up to stroke the damaged wing and reassure her.

The hope that they could stay undiscovered until she released Gideon was out the window now. The explosion did have the bonus that now all the Rosh barkers wandering around rushed towards the airship. She would skin Talen if he let them destroy her ship. She couldn't worry about that now as she had a troublesome dragon to find.

Hara waited for the revolutionaries to run past before she approached the barn. She should have picked up a gun, she realised as the only weapon she had were her wits and Angel.

She didn't go for the front door, but rather one of the side doors. Definitely not a farming building anymore as this had a large ramp up to it made from slates of metal, which would be completely impractical for animals. The gear once used to move hay around was merely a hole in the roof. The Rosh Barkers had been here long enough to settle in, it seemed.

Hara pressed her ear to the door. She could hear Gideon talking to someone so he wasn't alone. She was quiet as she picked the lock. It was sophisticated enough that it took a while and probably the reason why they had no guard on this door. They probably put it in for convenience and then had forgotten about it after they had finished using it.

Hara winced when the door made a loud click as the door opened. She waited a moment, but when

Gideon still continued to natter on, she knew they hadn't heard the click. She opened the door slowly, with Angel leaning forward so she could see into the barn first.

Inside there was a large crossbow like thing. The arms of the bow structure stood on a mobile base and it was massive. Taking up most of the barn with the large span. Gideon was on top of it, on what seemed like a compact steam engine, which she assumed wound the whole contraption up to shoot.

Gideon was talking to Nikolai, who was watching him work. The leader of the Rosh Barkers was alone. Thank goodness for small mercies. He also didn't seem at all phased by the yelling and explosions from outside. Nikolai was completely focused on Gideon.

Hara picked up a wrench left by a lazy worker and snuck up nearer to Nikolai. Angel jumped off her shoulder and landed on the ground clumsily. Hara would have to fix her wing before she could glide properly. She scuttled off, but Hara wasn't concerned, Angel had already proven that she could look after herself.

Nikolai stood too far away from anything for her to sneak up completely to him without him noticing her. And she still had her glider on her back, which didn't make her the best at sneaking.

Angel had somehow managed to get up on the machine and trilled at Gideon.

Nikolai looked towards the machine, giving her the distraction she needed to move. She swung the wrench as she ran. Nikolai must have seen the movement as he turned towards her at the last second. The momentum of her swing forced past his raised arm and she managed to knock him back. She

124

swung again, this time there was a crack and Nikolai grunted in pain.

He reached out with his other hand and grabbed her arm. She had expected this and instead of fighting, she stepped in closer and with her other hand, she jabbed him in his throat. He let her go in pain and this time she brought the wrench down on his head and stumbled the rest of the way to the ground. Unconscious most likely, but she had panicked and she might have hit him too hard.

Hara turned to Gideon, who was working feverishly. She frowned, but didn't question it. She climbed up the contraption. "We need to get out of here." And offered her arm to Angel, who quickly scrambled up and wrapped itself around her neck.

Gideon finished what he was doing. "I'd say. This place is going to blow. In about 26 seconds."

That was when she realised he had set the boiler on the machine to overheat and blow. The needle on the pressure gauge was building up too fast. She swore.

Gideon put his hands out and she undid the bands without having to be asked. He threw them away. She hadn't taken into account that he would be increasing his mass when he became a dragon.

Hara scrambled off the machine as blue light filled the barn. A large claw caught her as she stumbled off the edge when she had gone too far, blinded by the light. Angel twittered angrily at the sudden movement. Hara opened her eyes and saw through the white spots floating in her eyes that Gideon had changed completely into his gold dragon self.

He had her curled up against his chest as he pushed away from the ground and through the roof of the barn. Wood splintered around them and was soon followed by a massive explosion which took out the rest of the barn. They were already gaining altitude.

Hara managed to tug down her goggles so she could see without her eyeballs being blasted. She looked around for the Blazing Blunderbuss and swore when she saw it wasn't where she had left it. The ship was limping away from the hamlet.

Gideon changed his course and headed for the airship. He grabbed onto the ship and it tipped with his weight. He placed her on the deck. Light filled her vision and she turned her head away as he changed. She turned back when the light disappeared.

Gideon pulled himself up over the railing and onto the ship. She caught his arm and helped him up over. He stood up, but didn't let her pull away.

He tugged her closer and she let him. He asked, "You came for me." Angel twittered harshly. Obviously, she hated being left out. Gideon reached up and brushed a finger over her head. "And you too."

Hara frowned. "Of course. I wasn't about to leave you fixing a weapon for a bunch of Rosh Barkers. Besides, we are still short crewed and we'll need you if we want to escape."

Gideon grinned with the corner of his mouth. "You came to me because you like me."

Hara rolled her eyes and tugged herself free of him. "In your dreams, Gideon."

He cheekily said to her back as she stormed off to see how the crew were doing. "Every night. You know that."

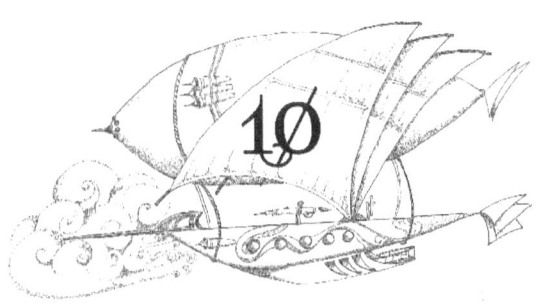

Hara found Gideon in her room working on something. She said, "You know you have a perfectly good room of your own."

Gideon didn't look up from his equations as he said, "I like yours better."

She closed the door behind her as she entered the room. She sat on the bed as he was on the only chair in the room. She crossed her legs and watched him for a while. "The Rosh Barkers won't bother us anymore."

Angel hopped onto her lap. Her wing was already fixed and better than ever. Angel had gotten very affectionate after the repair and Hara let her cuddle in her lap.

Gideon was very perceptive as he wasn't fooled by her prevarication. "I'm not going back."

Hara sighed. "Why not? You don't have to worry about being kidnapped anymore." There went that hope though she knew her heart wasn't really into getting rid of him.

"Because you are in my collection." His answer annoyed her.

She shook her head. "Not yet."

Gideon looked up at her. His eyes flashing with his emotions. "I think I am growing on you. So I believe

I will stick around until you can't think of me being anywhere else." His tone grew serious. "I know everyone in your life goes away. You are just pushing me away to protect yourself. So I'm going to stick around. Regardless."

Hara wrinkled her nose. He might be right and there was no way to make him stay in his own home in any case. He had wings and could follow her anywhere.

She pulled her knees up to her chin. "My father is not someone you want to add to your collection Gideon. He is a con man and he uses people. Especially people he thinks are family."

Gideon turned around and rested his arm on his leg. "I am aware of your father's flaws. I still don't think that will change my mind."

Her thoughts were confused. She wasn't sure if she wanted him to be so stubborn or not. He tilted his head and studied her for a while before he said, "Where I come from we are hatched. My mother and father were not present at my birth. In fact, neither of them acknowledges me. I have plenty of siblings, but again, none of them care to know about me. I know what it is like to have a family who wishes you weren't part of them. While they still think they can use you. You met Harlen. Well, he is my brother and all he wants from me is to make me a puppet. For him and his Emperor."

Hara snorted ungracefully. "Harlen is tame compared to my father. Trust me. When you meet him, you will want to run in the opposite direction."

Gideon smirked. "Ah, a bet I can win."

She wasn't sure what he meant by that and she was too tired to try get the answer out of him.

Gideon sat on the bridge watching the scenery. Alice glanced around to make sure no one else approached him.

She asked, "Hey, Gideon is it true?"

He glanced back at Hara's Alice and asked, "What is true?"

Alice twisted her hands in her gray smock. "That you are a dragon."

He turned to look at her fully before he said, "And if I was a dragon what would that mean?"

Her hands were completely twisted up in her clothes now. "Nothing, it is just I have never met a dragon before."

Gideon tilted his head to the side as he studied Alice.

He asked curious, "I have met many lately who have never met a dragon before. This is curious to me. When we first came to walk amongst you after the treaty everyone seemed to recognise us. What has changed?"

Alice shrugged and gave a guess. "Maybe it is because you don't eat us no more. I mean people are always aware of things which are dangerous."

Gideon flashed his teeth. "If only it was that easy."

Alice turned slightly to go back to her post but hesitated. She smoothed out the wrinkles in her skirt, then finally said, "Are you going to make Hara part of your collection? I've heard Dragons like to collect women. And that is why we used to put out women to appease the dragons in the days before the treaty."

Gideon shook his head. "That wasn't why you guys did that. We used to eat the women. But one was

129

rather charming and told us stories, so we kept her. We started keeping the women because they were interesting. It was later we figured out we had a use for women other than entertainment. That is when we made the treaty."

Alice shrugged, she wasn't blind to how men saw women and it didn't surprise her that women were the preferred sacrifice. She asked, "But what about Hara?"

Gideon smiled. "Oh, we are in negotiations."

Alice laughed. "I didn't know dragons negotiated with their collections."

Gideon wiggled his eyebrows. "Only the good ones."

Hara couldn't sit down so she paced. This had all been a complete mess. They had escaped the Rosh Barkers and Talen was the only one injured. He sat with his arm tucked up against his chest. Alice had patched him up but Hara felt more than just a little guilty.

If she hadn't stuck her nose into Gideon's problems at the start of all this, they wouldn't have had to face the Rosh Barkers.

Hara stopped pacing. "I can take you guys anywhere you want to go."

Alice frowned. "But I like it here. You have given me responsibilities and you are teaching me things. In my old town my dad always made me do woman's stuff. I'm not going anywhere."

Hara looked at Liam. He flushed as he had been caught looking at Alice.

Liam cleared his throat. "I got nowhere to go. This place is as good as anywhere else."

What he didn't say was he had a crush on Alice and would stick around. Hara sighed. She also understood that at his age there was a danger for him out on his own. Trouble would be chasing his heels just as it had in his home town.

Hara looked at her gunner, Murphy, and Henry.

Henry shrugged. "I'm still thinking about it. I like cooking. Doesn't really matter where."

Murphy crossed his arms across his chest and then relaxed his bravado and admitted honestly. "Man, Hara you have some of the nicest guns out there."

The men in the room all said, "Hey!"

Murphy's ears went red and he said, "I mean real guns. Get your minds out of the gutter guys. If someone else can offer me better ordinance, then I might move on but I like the guns so I'll stick around."

Hara turned to Talen. His eyes sparked. "For now I'll stay. I'm waiting for some word about a score. When that comes in I'll move on but till then I'll keep you company."

His eyes went to Gideon and she knew he would stay to make sure she didn't get too close to Gideon. He really didn't have anything to worry about. Not that she didn't have feelings for the dragon, but because it had nothing to do with Talen. That was an issue she would settle another day. The others left to go to their work, but she stopped Talen.

He sighed. "Okay, I'll be honest, I don't trust that dragon and we are a good team."

Talen went to leave again and she tightened her hand on his arm. "That dragon has saved my life. I trust him more than I would trust my own father."

131

Hara raised her eyebrows and added, "Do you understand? You are not my father and you don't have to protect me. I have been looking after myself since my father realised I was useful and dragged me off to play darling for some minor court."

Talen pursed his lips, then nodded his head sharply. "I understand."

———————————◆———————————

The weather was hot, but not so astonishing in the Mediterranean. The island they were on was a busy port and Hara was hoping to pick up a decent cargo. Gideon, her constant shadow was looking around as he followed her. He and Angel had come to some agreement as Angel watched out one way and he the other.

Gideon said conversationally, "I think I like the sunshine. Never get much of it in the capital. Though I really can't blame geography for that. I didn't leave the campus very often."

Hara glanced over at him. "Do you miss it? I mean working with other academics and such. I don't think there are even books on the Blazing Blunderbuss."

Gideon shook his head. "I was bored so it was easier to keep my head down. This is by far more interesting. Mmm, but I think we should get some books. The others would probably like a library. I did find some books in my room, but none of them are appropriate for the young impressionable minds on the ship. Who would have guessed pirates would be so smutty."

Hara knew Alice would appreciate some books. She was educated and though she had to leave everything she knew behind it would be nice to give her something of home while they travelled. It also might be a good idea to teach Liam how to read and write. Hara was already teaching him how to keep up the engine on the Blazing Blunderbuss but he would need to be able to read and write to go to the next level. Though maybe she could con Gideon into teaching the boy.

Liam was good with numbers and Gideon might be able to put off his dislike of human beings long enough to teach the boy.

Hara didn't know about Henry. He could have taken a job here or any other place they had stopped recently, but he always managed to come up with another excuse for why he would stay with the ship a little longer. Hara thought he had the same problem as her. She had always felt she had nowhere where she belonged, until the Blazing Blunderbuss. She could be herself and not worry about what others thought.

Hara knew she would have to thank Gideon for that someday, but she knew if she thanked him now, he would be insufferably smug for days. She was just about to say something when Angel called out a warning and Gideon shoved her.

Hara stumbled and turned to glare at him, but he wasn't there, he was running. She chased after him and saw he was chasing someone. She pulled out her gun and aimed at a rope which was holding up an awning just in front of the running men. She shot and cut the rope. The awning fell and tangled up with the running man.

Gideon jumped on him. When she approached, he had the man facing up, and sitting on the man's chest.

Gideon growled. "Why were you shooting at us?"

It was then she noticed the cross bow tucked into the man's belt. A little archaic, but it had been silent. A shiver went down her spine. That shove had probably saved her life.

The assassin smashed his head forward, surprising Gideon. He shoved Gideon and he fell into a bucket of pig's blood. The man managed to get a knife and she went to shoot the man, but the assassin pulled a woman against his chest and pressed the knife to her throat. Hara put her gun down and the assassin let the woman go and turned and ran.

Gideon made a disgusted sound. "Argh, are we going to go after him?" He tried to clean himself off but the blood had soaked into his clothes.

Hara shook her head. Assassins weren't the kind to tell their secrets. She caught Gideon's arm. "I'm afraid we can't stick around to find out. Someone would have heard this commotion."

He blinked, confused for a moment. "But he was the assassin."

Angel trilled in agreement with Gideon. Even though Gideon was older than her he was sometimes naive. "Yes, and I'm sure they will be happy to listen to us while they throw us into a prison."

He shrugged and followed after her. Gideon asked, "Why do you think he attacked?"

"I don't know and that worries me more." She tugged on his arm as she spoke. Her eyes kept a watch for people who were paying too much attention to them. This wasn't something new to her.

Gideon seemed unconcerned. "Oh, why is that?"

Someone ducked their head away, making her look at them, but they were closing up their shutters. There was nothing to fear from them.

"Well, if it were the Rosh Barkers then I know where to go to hurt them, but since you blew up their weapon they seem to have cut their losses," Hara said distractedly.

Gideon asked with a small frown. "Are you sure this isn't the Rosh Barkers? We did blow up their fancy little weapon after all."

Hara shook her head and placed her hand on his chest to stop him from stepping out of the alleyway. A few soldiers rushed past and she motioned when it was clear again. "No, it wasn't the Rosh Barkers. They were pawns of the Rosh Government. With that plan not viable, they will find their funding drying up very quickly. The Rosh won't want the Barkers to have free rein. So, though they might still be around they don't have the funding to send assassins after us. No, we don't have to worry about the Rosh Barkers."

They were almost to the Blazing Blunderbuss. "Oh, I didn't realise they were working for the Rosh Government. Mmm, that is a dangerous game. Using people like pawns like that," Gideon said speculatively.

Hara didn't disagree, but it wouldn't be the first time a government used people. "A desperate game. The Rosh doesn't want to be consumed by the Empire."

Gideon shrugged. "Most countries say that, but over time they don't particularly care who the government is as long as they are looked after. The Empire will only go after Rosh if they believe the Government is ineffective. At the moment they are effective, so they have nothing to worry about."

Hara turned to glance at him. "You know that?"

135

He nodded and explained, "If the Empire decided it needed more land it would finish eating up the Middle East."

Hara had to agree there. That would take a while and she wondered if the Empire would go after something easier in the meantime. But if Gideon was right, they would only go after weak countries and Rosh was far from weak.

They reached the Blazing Blunderbuss and she called up for the ladder. For the moment all they would care about was staying out of an island prison and the sights of assassins.

———◆———

Talen watched as Hara dumped Gideon's clothes in a bucket. Hara was determined not to look in the room where he was changing though he had kindly left the door open to tempt her. They had played this game often over the weeks they had travelled.

Talen raised an eyebrow, but she waved off his concern. He shrugged and asked, "I know someone who might be able to tell me who is after you."

He glanced at the open door and added, "Though the lizard seemed to keep you safe."

Angel trilled angrily as if to disagree. Hara reached up and patted the small dragon. "I know you helped as well, Angel." She frowned at Talen. "He is a dragon not a lizard. They don't even come from this planet. Wait, are you still not over that."

Talen shrugged. "I know dragons and their collections. They are possessive and obsessed with people in their collections. You know that is what he wants from you."

Her anger was fast and burned hot. Why did Talen insist on trying to protect her from the wrong things? He had never been like this with her father and he had done more harm to her in one day than Gideon had done in the entire time she had known him.

"Yes, and he has been open about all that crap. But why are you upset about it? My dad used to use me all the time and he couldn't care less what happened to me. Are you saying that a neglectful and careless person is better than a possessive and obsessive one?"

His eyes sparked. "Yes. At least you could get away from your dad. Once you are in a dragon's collection you will never be able to escape."

Hara leant against the wall and frowned as she thought over his words. "You think he is going to hurt me. Try to control me?" That at least was clear and she admitted to Talen honestly. "I'm worried about that, but you make it sound like it might get physical."

Talen was tense. "You don't? If you want to leave what will happen?"

She pushed a stick through the bucket to give it a swirl before going back to lean against the wall. "Nothing, well he might whine. But if I wanted to walk away, he would do nothing to stop me."

Gideon popped his head around the door. "I'd whine excessively. Oh and flowers, I'd definitely try flowers."

Hara rolled her eyes as Gideon finished dressing and came out into the corridor. He tucked in his shirt tails. "I wouldn't hurt her. The whole point of this following around behind her and all is to prove to her

I ain't like her dear old poppy. What about you, Talen? Are you nothing like her dad?"

She shot Gideon a look, then decided to change the subject and said to Talen, "Go ask your friend about the assassin and see if you can find out who is trying to kill me. I don't like not knowing who my enemies are."

Talen glared at Gideon, but he pushed away from the wall and stalked away. Gideon seemed oblivious to the glare as he picked up the bucket with his clothes and trotted off to deal with them. At least he cleaned up after himself. That was already better than her father.

———————◆———————

Hara was on duty when Talen returned. She threw the ladder down and leant on the railing as he climbed up. She waited for him to have both his feet on the deck when she asked, "Did you find out who hired the assassin?"

Talen nodded and leant back on the railing. He crossed his arms. "You're not going to like it."

Hara raised an eyebrow. "Someone is trying to kill me, I don't think it really matters who it is, I'm not going to like it."

He twitched his nose. "Well, my friend says that it is the Rosh Government and the name on the kill list is not yours but Captain of the Blazing Blunderbuss."

Hara swore. "I knew that would bite me on the ass. Well, did your friend have anything else to say?"

Talen hesitated and asked, "Are you really thinking about shacking up with the dragon?"

She sighed. She knew she wouldn't be able to avoid this conversation. "I'm not sure Talen. I like him and he is amusing, but I'm still thinking. I'm not going to rush into anything. At least Gideon is letting me have time. I don't see why it is your problem."

His face looked dark as he asked, "What would your dad say?"

Hara growled. "My dad can go to hell. I don't care what he thinks anymore. You know he left me in prison, Talen. He left me to rot. It was pure luck I impressed the judge and he gave me a second chance. My dad wasn't anywhere when that happened. So I don't care what my poor old daddy thinks."

She stormed off. She saw Gideon waiting, but he didn't say anything. He followed her to her room. "What is going to happen now?"

Hara shook her head. "I don't know Gideon. I still need time."

He shook his head. "No, I mean about the assassin."

She let out a breathy chuckle. "I think I'll have to beard the dragon in its own den."

Gideon chuckled. "Sounds like a plan. Now are we talking about the assassin or about me?"

She laughed and closed the door on his face.

Gideon sat on the stool she had placed at the front of the bridge. It was his favourite spot to look out. She knew it was because he was used to seeing where he was going while he flew. If they ever needed him, it would be as his dragon form not his human form. Angel sat with him and the two of them were watching the world pass by beneath them.

Gideon turned to Hara. "Are you sure about this? The Rosh hasn't treated us well recently. They kidnapped me. Twice."

She couldn't disagree with him, but she hated hidden dangers like this. She would rather face her problems than hide.

Hara had done enough of that already. "It is the only way we'll be able to protect ourselves in the long run Gideon. We have had this conversation before."

That had been at the border when they had made contact with a Rosh agent who had set up the meet. They were to meet with a Rosh member of parliament who was in charge of foreign relations. Hara assumed that was just a euphemism as the Rosh didn't play well with others even on a good day.

Gideon turned back to look over Moscow. He said softly but she heard him. "I don't trust them."

But they didn't have much choice. Either they faced their problems or they would never be able to sleep. Talen added his two cents worth and said, "With the way you travel you might be able to stay ahead of them for a while."

Hara shook her head. "They would just need to place an assassin in each port. And the Rosh are rich enough to do that. No, we have to face them to be safe."

Murphy said, "You sure you don't want me there with my girls." He patted the guns at his hips to indicate he meant his weapons.

She shook her head. "I'm trying to stop people from wanting to kill me not give them another reason by introducing you to them."

Murphy grinned at her but didn't disagree.

Snow fell in soft flurries. It was cold but stalls were still calling out their wares so Hara assumed weather like this was common in Moscow with the amount of people still on the streets as they walked through a marketplace. Hara patted her arms. "I really should get one of those coats. They sure do look warm." They appeared to be made from fur from some sort of small animal.

Gideon said, "I can get you a coat."

She shook her head. "We can't afford a coat. We hardly have enough money to pay for supplies."

Gideon shook his head and flicked his hand and a rose appeared.

Hara jumped. "How did you do that? Sleight of hand? I thought you dragons only had your hoard in whatever place you make things pop out from."

She took the flower and looked it over carefully.

It was made of silk and Gideon said sadly, "Sorry, real flowers don't really have the staying power in the space between planes."

She blinked and asked, "What are you talking about?"

He guided her towards a stall with coats as he said, "Our people travelled here from another place. Have you ever seen a creature on your planet which has four legs and wings? No, because we don't come from here. We have found a way to manipulate the natural world. We can fold time and space. Though not always."

Hara frowned. "The bracelets?"

Gideon smiled. She really was clever. He stopped her in front of the stall of fur coats. "Pick one. It is a gift. No strings attached."

She shook her head. "You already put money down for the ship."

His gold eyes sparked with emotion. "And I would pay it again. I have lived a long time and I have collected a large amount of wealth. You do not have to worry about money, my dear."

Hara shook her head. "It is your money not mine."

He lifted a beautiful gray fur coat off a stand and draped it over her shoulders.

Hara said as she tucked her hands in the pockets. "It is a man's coat."

"It looks good on you." She took her hand hands out of the pockets to smooth her hand over the fur. Before she could come up with an excuse not to buy it, he flicked his fingers and dropped some coins on the table of the stall owner. The coins disappeared as quickly as they appeared. Hara thought about complaining but the coat was very warm and it really was cold. If she thought Gideon expected anything from her, she would have put the coat back regardless of the money exchanged.

Gideon placed his hands into his pockets and she asked as they walked away. "Aren't you cold?"

Gideon tapped his chest. "I have my own heat."

Hara huffed, but didn't say anything about the coat. "You are insufferable, Gideon."

He grinned at her. "If that were true you wouldn't be here."

"Now I know why your mother abandoned your egg." The words were harsh but there was amusement in her voice.

Gideon bumped his shoulder with hers as he said, "So I could be free to fly on my own."

The warehouse where they were to meet Marya their contact was mostly empty when they entered. Gideon behind her look around.

He sniffed. "It smells like tea in here."

A voice further into the warehouse said, "Darjeeling to be exact."

A woman stepped out from behind a large crate. She was an older lady, but still stunning. Her hair up in a loose bun. Her hands were tucked into a large fur coat.

The woman added, "I was under the impression you would be alone."

Hara sighed. They had argued about this on the ship but no one had been comfortable with her going alone. "He is a dragon there is no way to make him do anything he doesn't want to do."

Marya tilted her head sideways as she studied Gideon. "I had heard you spent time with dragons. I thought they were merely rumours. Interesting." Marya came closer. This time her gaze was on Hara. "So you are the one who stole my airship."

Hara wasn't about to let this woman guilt trip her. "Yeah, sorry about that. We have money."

Marya stopped in front of them. She was a very small woman for her presence. "That isn't how it works. That ship was meant to play a particular part in our own interests. Selling it to you isn't in our interests."

Hara frowned. She had hoped they could buy off the Roshians as easily as it had been to buy off the pirates.

Hara finally said, "Well, I had hoped to settle all this as I'm tired of assassins."

Marya's eyebrow twitched and she said calmly, "The Rosh government does not deal in assassins."

Hara waved it off. "I don't care what the policy is for assassins, I just don't want to kill some sad sods because they decided to take a contract on me."

Marya pulled her hands out of her coat and laid a roll of paper on a low crate. She asked, "Do you know what this is?"

Gideon answered, "It is the writ of Transport. Well, a copy. It is very pretty with all those curly letters. All the countries in the world signed it."

Marya seemed impressed then asked, "You were there?"

He nodded. "It was a great party. They had quail inside of ducks for the main course."

Marya ignored his comments and motioned to the scroll. "That also allows for the commission of Privateers. The Blazing Blunderbuss has been commissioned as a privateer. That is our right. We don't particularly like people flying around in our ships and not working for us. So are we going to have a deal here? The Blazing Blunderbuss has a letter of Marque and her job isn't finished."

Gideon glared at the woman. Hara said, "Let me have a moment here with my associate and I'll have your answer in a jiffy."

The woman shrugged and sauntered off with her hands back in her pockets. Gideon turned to her and hissed in a loud whisper. "You can't seriously be thinking about becoming a pirate."

Hara shrugged. "I don't want to but what choice do we have? We will pick targets who are picking on other ships. We'll clean up the skies. Help others."

Gideon rolled his eyes. "You are away with the fairies if you believe that for a moment."

Hara asked him, "If we go through with this, will you stay?" Her heart actually went into her throat at the thought of him leaving. She wasn't ready to lose him yet.

Gideon turned his back to her. "I don't know."

Marya must have sensed they had come to the end of their conversation as she returned. "So do you have an answer?"

Hara gritted her teeth. "You know we don't really have a choice."

Marya gave a warm smile which was more tooth than truth. "Good. Here is your first target." Hara hesitated, but took the piece of paper Marya offered. Hara looked at the location and the name of the ship.

Marya said, "If I don't hear about the demise of this ship be sure that you will have trouble shortly afterwards." She turned and started walking away and she said over her shoulder. "Kale isn't the only one good at infiltration."

If Hara wanted confirmation that the Rosh government had been behind the Rosh Barkers she knew now Marya had her hand in that particular pie. Marya added conversationally, "Oh, and your granddad's place is adorable."

With that Marya was gone. Gideon was red with anger. His fists clenched.

Hara touched her shoulder where Angel came out to click her concern. Hara asked, "Gideon?"

"I will kill her and eat her."

Trust a dragon to first jump to violence to solve the issue. Or was it just a male thing? "That won't work, she is the hand of a monster. She isn't the monster itself." She tugged at him and said, "Come we need to get there fast otherwise we are in trouble."

Gideon growled. "You are going attack an innocent ship?"

Hara wasn't sure yet what she was going to do. One thing was sure, she would do everything to keep her crew safe. "I don't know, but I'm going to be there and I'll make my choices as they come along."

Gideon looked dark.

Hara touched his arm. "I swear I'll only attack if they are the villain. If they are innocent, I'll leave them alone. We'll do what Talen suggested and run. We'll pick up Opa and make him come along and we will disappear to the other side of the world and the Rosh can go stuff themselves."

Gideon's look was still dark, but he was now thoughtful. He said after a long moment. "You swear."

"Yes. I'm not a murderer." But she had been the cause of deaths. Nikolai was almost assuredly dead from that explosion and she had known Kale was killed in the skirmish. She had known that was his fate when she had left him to Talen. She might not have blown up the boiler on the weapon or put the knife in Kale's gut, but they were dead because of her.

The judge who had taken pity on her had helped her come to terms with the people who had died in her past. That made her more aware now of all the people's lives in her hands. Regardless of whether she pulled the trigger or not.

"You need to trust me, Gideon."

He nodded his head sharply and stormed ahead. She let him have his space for a while. When his pace slowed down she approached him. He was still fuming. She said, "I won't make you kill humans."

Gideon stopped completely and turned to look at her. He said, "I never thought you would."

"Good." At least they were on the same page about something.

He frowned for a long moment, then said, "With the other dragons they never understood that. Never understood I can't take lives like that."

Hara said softly, "You have killed, you know." His eyes went stormy and she added, "Nikolai was in that barn when you blew it up. There were others outside. They most likely died. All our actions have consequences. Some minor and some which are deadly. I was part of Nikolai's death. If I hadn't knocked him out, he might have been able to pull himself out of there. I know when I put a man at the guns that one of those bullets could end a life or many lives. It is never done lightly. I will do everything in my power to preserve life. You understand that?"

Gideon surprised her by pulling her in for a kiss. She resisted for a moment because she was startled by the move. But she enjoyed the way his lips felt on hers. She put her arms around his neck and moved closer.

He stopped after a moment and his eyes studied her face for a long moment. He then said, "We should get back. And it is now your turn."

It took her a moment to realise what he meant but remembered how she had kissed him the other day. Hara nodded, though she wasn't in any rush to move her arms away from his neck.

———————

Gideon was very quiet as they approached the map coordinates Marya had given them. They were a little early so Hara wasn't really looking for an airship.

Hara came to stand next to him and asked, "Gideon?"

He turned to look at her. "I have lived a very long time and I have realised my hands are not as clean as I had thought."

She winced. That had not been the point of her speech in Moscow. But she hated thinking of him in any way the villain.

Alice yelled and pointed. Their conversation would have to wait. The ship they were supposed to take was coming slowly around a mountain. Very slowly in fact. She would have said it was drifting by the way it was moving.

Hara reached over for the telescope and extended it out to its full length before placing it to her eye.

There were a lot of people crowded on the deck. A plank stretched out and the crowd was forcing a man to walk the plank. She swore and focused on the man. That garish red coat looked a little familiar.

She dropped her hand down with the telescope when she realised who the man was.

Hara called urgently, "Talen!"

Talen approached and asked, "What do you need?"

She passed him the telescope. "Please tell me that isn't my dad."

Talen's face showed all the anguish she felt. He didn't hesitate to look through the telescope.

He didn't look for long before he lowered the telescope. "I'm afraid it is him. What do you think? Marvin has been up to his usual tactics?"

Hara shook her head, but not to his question. "It doesn't matter. He is still my father, so we will rescue him."

Gideon said, "I'll get him."

She caught his arm and asked, "Are you sure?"

He knew what she was asking. By going after her father there was a good chance he would be forced to attack the ship. People might die and though the ship wasn't completely innocent because they were trying to kill her father she knew Gideon didn't want to kill people. She understood the other ship, she had wanted to kill her father a few times. They didn't deserve to die for that alone.

Gideon nodded his head and pulled away from her. She turned to the others. "Man the guns and Alice you take the wheel. Move the ship how I showed you."

Henry would help out Liam in the boiler room so they would have the power to move. She went to the guns on the left while Murphy went to the others.

Talen said, "I'll help Gideon."

She wasn't sure how he was going to do that, but it might be a good idea to have him there when

Gideon brought her father to the Blazing Blunderbuss.

Alice asked, "Are we really going to be pirates?"

The thought made Hara's throat feel like she had swallowed ash. "Today we are. They have my father, Alice."

Alice nodded. She understood family as well as Hara did. They needed to distract the ship so they wouldn't fire on Gideon. Hopefully to give him enough time to get close enough to save her father.

The other ship noticed them and she could see people moving on the deck. Gideon had changed and he flew up. He buzzed the airship making it shake. Her father tipped off the plank, but she saw Gideon dive for him. She saw they had men at their guns as the guns started to move.

Hara didn't wait for them to shoot at the Blazing Blunderbuss or at Gideon and opened fire. She aimed for the stabilisers on the side as she didn't want to kill the crew.

Marya hadn't said they had to take the cargo which was a usual thing for privateers so they would just damage the ship and hopefully buy themselves enough time to come up with a better solution than becoming pirates full time.

Something hit them and it made the airship tilt. Talen yelled. "Go, go, go."

It must mean Gideon was back. Alice spun the wheel and they turned away from the fight. The other ship was already limping and going down fast though only one of side of the envelope was deflated. It would be a while before they were airborne again.

Marvin, her father, walked onto the ship and waved his arms out. "Oh, wonderful, wonderful."

This was the first time Hara had seen him since he had left her and she realised she still wasn't ready to face him. She turned slowly away from him.

Marvin approached her and went to hug her, but she sidestepped him. She went to Alice and motioned for the girl to go to her usual position.

Gideon entered onto the bridge and came to stand by Hara.

Marvin frowned a little, but it didn't last very long on his face. He said, "Aren't you happy to see me, darling? You are certainly a blessing and your timing perfect. I was about to be a meat pancake on the side of some nameless mountain." He approached Gideon and patted his shoulder. "Thanks for the save. You can't imagine what I was thinking as I was falling. I truly thought it was the end of me."

Marvin patted his coat and pulled out a silver flask. He grinned as he screwed off the cap. "Ah, at least I left with the essentials."

Hara said to Talen, "Take him to one of the rooms. Settle him in. We'll talk later."

Talen nodded and guided Marvin off the bridge.

Gideon said, "Are you alright?"

Hara nodded. "I'll talk to him later when I'm not so mad."

He frowned at her tone, but didn't say anything.

━━━━━━━━━◆━━━━━━━━━◆━

Gideon watched as Hara concentrated on the maps. She had set the course already so there was no need for her to be so focussed. He knew it was her father. That man had more in common with dragons than was healthy.

If Hara had been without her Opa she doubted she would have survived past her childhood years. Marvin was callous as a snake. A trait his daughter did not share.

Gideon realised now she would never have killed those people even if the Rosh had threatened her. She was clever enough to find a third path. Maybe he should take a page out of her book and pick a third path. Marvin might be her father, but he wasn't in her collection and he wouldn't be in his. Marvin would be treated like a dragon father and he decided he didn't need to add him to his collection.

Gideon found Marvin lounging in the mess. He was cheery with liquor. Gideon sat down and poured himself a drink from Marvin's silver flask. The con man grinned at him. "Haven't seen a dragon in a long while. I tend to steer away from you types."

He tapped his temple. "You tend to be brighter than the average man. So what brings a bright spark like you to this ship?"

Gideon didn't prevaricate as he doubted subtly was Marvin's strong suit. "I'm here for your daughter."

Marvin grinned but he showed too many teeth. Marvin wasn't a friendly type. Gideon returned the grin also showing too much teeth. "You should see my real teeth."

Marvin's eyes sparked. He recognised the threat. Gideon left the drink on the table and left.

Hara knew she had to talk to her father, though she really wanted to be childish and just run to her bed and throw herself on it and cry. Unfortunately, she had to be the adult in the relationship. It had always been that way.

She knocked on the door and waited a second before she entered. Her dad lounged on his bed with his hands tucked behind his head. The casualness was too suspicious. She quickly looked around and saw he had been hiding something in the cavity behind the drawers as they were still slightly open. When her father looked too innocent there was always something he was hiding.

Hara would check it out later. Right now she had to get some answers from her father.

Marvin smiled at her. "You are looking good. I like the clothes. More feminine but still practical. I wonder why you didn't dress more like a girl when you were younger."

Not that her current outfit of leather pants and a blousy white shirt was very feminine. He meant her curves. She wasn't hiding them anymore.

He always did this selective memory. It hurt more than she realised as his actions had such an impact on her, but she knew she was barely a bump on his road. "Because you were taking me to dangerous places for girls, so I had to dress like a boy."

"Oh. Where was that?" He frowned in confusion.

Hara wasn't surprised he didn't remember. He wouldn't change. She waved it off, they weren't here to discuss the past. "How did you end up on that ship, dad?"

He settled more comfortably on his bed and pulled out his silver flask from under his hip. "Well, I needed to get to Siberia and they were heading that way. So I hitched a ride. But the captain wasn't very happy about the whole arrangement and that is when you found me. Good timing on that by the way."

"The Rosh government sent us." Hara wondered if it would worry him if she was working for the Rosh Government instead of the Empire. She didn't tell him she had been sent as a privateer as that was her own private shame.

Instead Marvin's grin brightened. "Perfect. The reason why I need to get to Siberia is I have to pick up something and take it to Moscow. You can stop in at Siberia for me and my project will go ahead as I planned."

Hara shook her head. He always had a plan or a deal going. She wasn't astonished that he hadn't changed. "What about our last project, dad? Did that go as you planned?" The bitterness of his betrayal tainted her voice.

Marvin rubbed his chin. "What about it? We got out with the money."

"You. You got out with the money. You left me there."

He frowned as he dredged his memory and then finally shook his head. "I was sure you had gotten out. Where have you been by the way? I went back to the workshop and you weren't there."

Hara wanted to hurt him for being such a careless rogue. She wanted him to feel the betrayal she had felt so she said, "Prison."

That had been true for a short time. It would have been a permanent reality if it had not been for a generous judge. Marvin gasped and jumped off the bed. "Oh, my dear, that is terrible."

He reached out to her for some comfort offered way too late. She stepped out of his reach. The offer wasn't an honest one in any case, he just wanted to bring her back under his thumb.

Hara closed her eyes because she had heard these words before. When she had to leave a place without a treasured item or when she had to leave a friend behind. She had learnt the hard way that those words were merely tools for her father to get what he wanted. And right then all he wanted was a ride.

Hara sighed and opened her eyes. She said, "I'll take you where you need to go, but after Moscow I don't want to see you again."

Marvin waved off her words. Probably sure he could convince her at some later date. But this was the last favour she would do for him and it was for her. As closure. He didn't realise it, but this trip wasn't a gift for her father it was merely for a client. He wasn't family anymore. She said her good nights to him and stepped out of his room.

Hara wasn't surprised to see Gideon had been waiting for her. He asked, "How are you?" She shrugged and he raised an eyebrow. "That bad?"

Tears pricked her eyes, but she refused to let them fall.

Gideon said, "I've met your father now."

Hara chuckled and let her mood improve a little. She asked, though she already knew the answer. "Are you still thinking of adding me to your collection?"

Gideon tugged on her arm and pulled her into his arms. He didn't try to kiss as it was still her turn to kiss him first but he laid his hands lightly on her waist. "I would give up everything else in my collection just to have you."

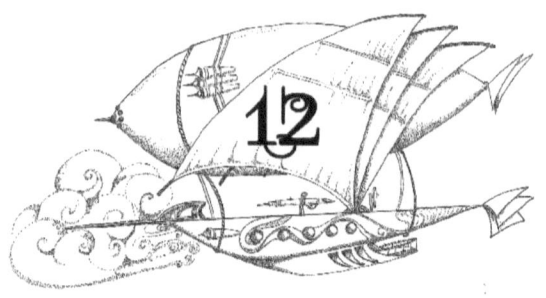

Hara moved carefully. Angel was asleep in a small ball on her pillow. Hara didn't want to wake the creature up as she had some plans for the night and didn't want company. The airship was quiet as Hara moved down the corridors.

She jumped when Gideon appeared in front of her. She rolled her eyes. She really should get used to him doing that. It was hours since the last time she had seen him and she had waited for him to go to bed before she had made her move.

Hara sighed. "Just be quiet." Considering he had managed to sneak up on her again she didn't doubt he could be quiet.

Gideon shrugged and followed behind her. He didn't ask what they were doing and just followed.

They went into her father's room. She took a dropper out of her tool belt and set a few drops on the pillow next to his head.

Her father snorted, but didn't stir. The drug would keep him in his sleep, but any loud noise could wake him up. She opened the drawer and the secret compartment. It contained a few letters.

Hara opened one and passed one to Gideon. She wasn't shocked when she saw it was a letter from a Rosh agent. It asked about a parcel and where it needed to be delivered. Her father really was working for the Rosh Government. He really didn't have any morals. The letter also said something about moving their efforts forward. How her father had gotten involved she could only imagine.

Gideon touched her shoulder and he showed her a letter. Hara blinked, startled. It was a love letter. Overly sappy to be honest, but she wouldn't have thought her father was the sentimental type to keep a lover or letters from her. The letters were signed by an M at the bottom.

Hara wondered who it could be. The letter from the Rosh government were probably the only sensitive information in the lot. She slipped the letters back into the secret compartment. Quietly the two of them left.

Near her room, Hara said softly. "I don't like any of this."

Gideon nodded in agreement. "Neither. But we'll have to let it play out." She knew he was right.

***

Hara was glad she had given in and let Gideon buy her a fur coat when they had been in Moscow. The snow worked in tight flurries around them as the ship moved through the air. The air itself had a sharp bite to it. So Hara had the fur coat tucked up around her neck.

Angel was tucked under the fur and was half wrapped around her ribs. The cold weather could be fatal to the small clockwork creature so Hara put up with her movement which tickled.

Hara asked her father who was standing next to her on the deck. "What the heck is here which hasn't frozen to a chunk of ice already?"

Marvin pointed to a small hut. "Over there. He should be waiting for us. Though he might have a bit of gear. That was what he said in his letters."

Hara could see some buildings in the distance. She tuned out her father as she really didn't want to hear about her father's latest deals. Besides more than half of his words were usually lies.

The Blazing Blunderbuss came to a stop near the buildings and Hara threw the rope ladder over the side. The others would come down in the slower lift, but she wanted to have a look at the agent first.

The buildings were mostly warehouses and a small cabin attached to the side of one of the warehouses. The door opened of the cabin and a man stepped out. He threw up his arms. "Where have you been? You were supposed to be here last week."

Hara looked over her shoulder and saw that her father had also come down on the rope ladder.

Marvin approached the agent and spoke to him soothingly. Hara followed them all into the house. Only to find it was a lab. The walls were white and the room was filled with metal tables with racks of test tubes on them. It was also freezing inside. Didn't the man heat the place?

The man was already collecting up his tools. He was throwing them haphazardly into a leather case. He said to her, "Make sure your men are careful with the case."

He motioned to a case sitting by the door. Marvin asked, "And the rest?"

The other man waved his hand dismissively. "Leave it. They have promised me a top of the line lab. This is all rubbish in comparison to what I will have when I get there."

Hara picked up the case herself. It wasn't heavy and it clinked with glass as she moved out of the cabin slash lab. Marvin said, "Well, let us be on our way Doctor."

The man corrected him by saying. "That is Professor."

Marvin laughed at his mistake. "Oh, that is right. Well, let us get you onto the airship and out of here straight away professor."

Hara doubted the man was a professor. He might have been at one time, but from the set up here in the middle of now where, she doubted he had a position anywhere. Let alone something as prestigious as a university professorship.

They all climbed onto the lift and she placed the case at her feet as she controlled the lift's rise to the airship. Angel twisted, tickling her. Hara resisted the urge to giggle. Everyone eyed her as she squirmed. When Angel settled Hara ignored the looks and set the lock of the lift.

The professor disappeared into the ship without waiting to be invited. Hara motioned to Talen and the man went after the Professor to make sure he didn't get lost.

Hara said to her father, "What is all this about?" She knew most of it from reading his letters, but she wanted to hear what he had to say.

Marvin shrugged, but she didn't believe for a moment he didn't know exactly what was going on.

She narrowed her eyes. "We are not going anywhere without some answers."

Hara motioned to the case at her feet. "Let's start with this."

Marvin wrinkled his nose and finally said, "It is a cure for what ails the world."

Hara was not fooled and asked, "And what ails the world?"

He glanced further into the ship. Probably looking out for someone. Anger dashed through her as she realised who he was looking for. "You mean dragons?"

Marvin's eyes shifted and he tucked his hands in his pockets.

Hara threw up her arms in the air. "You brought a poison for dragons on my ship where I so happen to have a dragon. A dragon who just saved your life two days ago. Are you crazy?"

He shook his head. "It will only be the dragons who attack Rosh. You work for them, so it won't be a problem."

Hara put out a hand to make him stop talking. She took a long breath. He had no idea. That was partly her fault. She could have told her father more about her rocky relationship with the Rosh Government. This poison would just give the Rosh one more piece of leverage to keep her working as a privateer. If the Empire ever found out she had played a part in this poison she would never be able to run to them for help. She would be alone in the world.

Hara waved for her father to leave. She crouched and picked up the case. She would store it in her room. There was no way she was going to let this leave her sight. It bugged her that the professor would leave it in her hands. He was a fool to trust her father or the Rosh. He was probably too busy drooling over the idea of a new lab to care who he was working for.

Once her father was gone, Gideon stepped out of the shadows. He didn't look pleased. He asked, "What are you going to do with that?"

Hara ignored his tone as she was angry as well and could understand his anger. She tucked the case under her arm. "Make sure it never sees the light of day. Walk with me while I put this away. Between the two of us, we can make sure it is never left alone."

He calmed down and nodded his head sharply.

———————————◆———————————

Gideon watched Hara sleep. She would probably be very mad with him if she caught him here. He grinned at the thought. But he wasn't here to admire her. He had a mission.

The case was easy to find. It was in a hidden safe under Hara's bed. It wasn't large and the lock was easy. He cracked it in a moment. He really missed this sometimes.

In the early days when he had refused to kill people, he had simply snuck into homes to take what he had needed. That was when he learned to appreciate the little things in life like a comfortable home.

He flipped the top of the case open. Inside was about fifty vials of a pale yellow liquid. He picked one up and tilted it to have a look at the substance inside. It looked like lemon juice and when he shook the vial it went clear. He had vials like these somewhere.

Gideon put the vials with its mates and closed the case. He wandered to the galley. Henry was sleeping in a hammock off the preparation area. He didn't stir as Gideon moved around.

Gideon took a few lemons and made enough liquid to fill fifty vials. He twisted his hand and brought the vials which had been in between places where dragons kept things to where he was in the Blazing Blunderbuss. He had stored them in his treasure room which really didn't exist in this world at all. But was mostly accessible from his apartment in the city.

He flipped his hair out of the way and filled the vials in precise movements. This wasn't the first time he had worked with vials and liquids. In his early days at Universities he had earned his way by working as a lab assistant.

Gideon cleaned up after himself and returned to Hara's room. She was no longer there. It had taken him longer to make the substitute poison. He wasn't concerned. He knew where she would be. She was on watch so he had time to move around her room. He replaced the vials and wondered what he could do with the real poison.

He took the vials and made them go in between space. It wasn't permanent, but it would do until he could figure out what to do with them.

◆━━━━━━━━━━◆

Hara knocked softly on the door. "Professor?" The doctor was writing something down and didn't look up, but motioned her inside. He reminded her of a real professor at that moment. She had assumed the title he insisted on was because he had once been a professor.

Curious, she asked, "What school by the way?"

The Professor looked up surprised. "Um the University of Prague. Not many people ask. How can I help you, Captain?"

Hara didn't go any further into his room, instead she leaned against the door. "That chest you had us bring along. I have put it under guard in my room. You want to tell me what is inside?"

He flicked a few pages and seemed to draw his attention away from the conversation as he said, "Well, it was supposed to be a virus which would make the human race more superior but instead it has an adverse effect on any dragon who has bonded with humans. Wasn't what I expected, but it will get me a new lab."

As Hara thought. He was amoral. All he cared for was recognition and in his mind that meant a fully kitted out lab. A very dangerous man indeed. Her father was a fool to deal with him.

Hara nodded her head to the Professor. "Thank you for appeasing my curiosity, Professor."

The professor beamed. "My pleasure."

When she stepped out of the Professor's room, she saw Gideon was waiting.

Hara smiled at him. "You are making a habit of this."

Gideon shrugged. "What did he have to say about the vials?"

She shook her head and the two of them walked to her room as she explained. "He is only looking out for himself. The poison is supposed to kill dragons with bonds to humans. An accident really. He was trying to make humans as strong as dragons."

Gideon wrinkled his nose. "Then I will be safe to watch it. But we can't let the vials or the professor or doctor, or whatever he is, get to the Rosh."

Hara smiled. "Should we throw him overboard?"

He chuckled as he knew she was joking and added, "I'll tie him up so he doesn't flail around."

She shook her head, enjoying the joke. "No, a gag." She sighed. "If only it was that simple." They were both quiet after that.

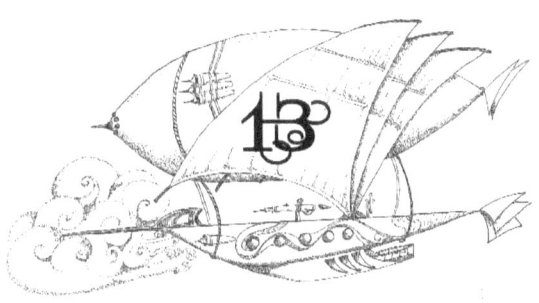

They all sat around the table in the mess. Liam was on watch but the rest sat around and tried Henry's French toast. Angel had curled up in a bowl on the table and people were careful not to disturb her. Hara didn't think a pirate attack could wake her. She had been watching the vials all night. Gideon was keeping an eye on them at the moment.

Alice said into the tense silence that reigned at the table, "This is good Henry."

Murphy humphed. "It needs meat."

Henry huffed. "Well, if you feel that way, then cook it yourself."

The Professor reached over and took Murphy's plate. Murphy went to reach for it back calling out. "Hey." But the Professor shoved the food into his mouth. Murphy's face twitched as he forced himself not to say anything.

Marvin laughed. "Not to worry Old man, have a bit of this." He offered his flask. Hara wondered where he always got his alcohol. They didn't have any on the ship as they had sold it to pay for supplies.

Murphy eyed it and then glanced at her. She wasn't sure what Murphy was asking, but after a long moment he shook his head and instead poured himself some more coffee.

Marvin peered closer at Angel. "What is this? I have an iron stomach, but ain't it strange to eat wire and gears like this."

Murphy answered, "It is a clockwork creature."

Marvin's eyes gleamed. He reached forward, but Hara intercepted him. "That is Angel and she is my friend. If you sell her I will hunt you down and take collateral out of your flesh."

Marvin put his hands up in mock fear. Hara narrowed her eyes and added, "I'm not fooling around, Marvin. I learnt a few things in prison and I will have no qualms about using what I learnt on you." She also wanted to remind him why she was still angry with him.

The Professor said, "What is the point? Those things are merely toys and useless in the grand scheme of things. Now if you had a flower that cured baldness or something. Now that would interesting." The professor continued on for a while about the benefits he had discovered in his studies.

Marvin pretended to ignore Angel but Hara knew she would have to watch him around her.

Something hit the side of the Blazing Blunderbuss. Hara didn't wait to see what it was as it was pitch black out there so there wouldn't be much to see.

Hara signalled to her people and they ran to their positions.

Her father asked with fear tinging his voice. "What about us?" He meant him and the Professor. She didn't think for a second that her father cared about what happened to her or to her crew.

Hara motioned them away. "Stay in my room. It's the most armoured place on the ship. Stay there until this is over. Lock the door."

It would also keep them out of their way as they dealt with whatever was attacking them. A large airship loomed out of the darkness. A little after they left Angel came flying out of the room. She went to land on Gideon's shoulder and chittered angrily at something outside the ship. Hara crossed the space and looked out the window to see what Angel and Gideon were looking at. Hara swore as she recognised it as an Empire dreadnaught. This was not good.

Someone said behind them, "This is actually nice."

Gideon growled and she turned to see it was the dragon who had been in Gideon's apartment when she had taken him home, Harlen.

Murphy pulled a gun, but she raised a hand to prevent him from shooting Gideon's brother or frenemy or whatever he was to Gideon. There was no love lost between the two, but she doubted Gideon wanted him dead.

The dragon, Harlen, looked around. "Where is the doctor?"

Hara sighed. There was one thing she realised about the Empire. They really were very well informed.

Gideon said, "In the Captain's room. Do you know what he is doing?"

Harlen nodded. "Yes and we have to stop him."

Hara liked that sentiment and stepped forward to address the dragon herself. "So are you going to deal with him and his poison?"

Harlen shrugged and she knew then it wasn't going to be something simple. The dragon said, "We can't let the Rosh think we have the doctor and the poison."

Hara sighed and looked at the ceiling as she prayed for some patience. She looked at the dragon. "What do you need?"

Murphy asked, "I thought we worked for the Rosh. Now we are going to do what the Empire wants?"

Hara said without turning to look at Murphy. "We don't work for either, Murphy. But if the Rosh get this doctor and his poison we will be going to war and no one will be safe."

She motioned for Harlen to continue. He said, "We need you to double cross the Rosh. Give them the poison and we will take the doctor. Get the doctor out on the deck in a short while. Make some excuse. We will take him. You carry on with the poison."

The dragon looked at Gideon, who simply nodded his head. The dragon tipped his head to her. "I'll be going now. We must make sure this little farce plays out right."

Harlen turned and left. The airship tipped and shuddered.

Hara motioned to Talen. "Get the Professor and my father onto the deck. My father needs to see this."

Talen asked, "And how am I supposed to do that? They are cowering like cowards under your bed."

Hara gritted her teeth at the image he elicited and answered. "Tell them there is a fire on the deck and that the rest of us are still fighting the Dreadnaught." A fire was a serious thing on an airship which was mostly made of wood and highly flammable materials.

Talen hesitated. "Are you sure about this?"

Hara nodded. It was the only way to save lives. She turned to the others. "Alice evasive manoeuvres."

Alice frowned, but nodded her head to accept the command. They weren't being shot at and the Dreadnaught was just sitting there. But her father would recognise the feel of an airship evading cannon fire.

Hara motioned to the others. "Stay here." Angel disagreed with a chirp and flew over to her shoulder. Hara patted her small paw.

Hara didn't trust the others to set a fire which looked believable and would do little damage. Gideon followed her. She could trust him. Besides, as a dragon he could probably put a fire out with just breathing on it in his dragon form. Or shifting it somewhere else like he had done with that silk flower.

Hara asked Gideon, "Are you going to do something about the poison?"

"Yes," he answered simply.

She nodded her head. There wasn't anything else to say on that topic.

Once on the deck Hara carefully set a fire. She made sure there was nothing close which was flammable. The last thing she wanted to do was burn her own airship to the ground. Angel made some hissing noise at the fire but remained on Hara's shoulder.

Hara looked at Gideon, and he answered without having to be asked. "The fire will burn out before it gets to anything flammable. If the wind was worse we would be in trouble."

Satisfied the fire would burn for a while and smoke enough to be convincing she turned and left.

Alice looked at her with a worried frown when they returned to the bridge. A small shake of Hara's head indicated to Alice to keep it to herself for the time being.

Hara nodded to Gideon and left to make sure Talen knew the plan and set the tone. On the Bridge they could hear the hurried steps of her father and the Professor as they raced to fight the fire. Hara called out some orders. Murphy frowned at her, but she shook her head. She would talk to them later.

When Talen got to the deck there would be a convincing fire for them to fight giving the dragon his opportunity to snatch away the Professor without any suspicion.

On the bridge Hara saw the dragon swoop past the large windows that wrapped around the front of the bridge. There was a short scream and she winced.

Alice asked, "They haven't killed him, have they?"

Hara shook her head. "If Gideon trusts them not to hurt him then I do as well." Alice frowned and Hara clarified, "The Professor is very good at making things. The Empire are not stupid enough to throw him away. The Professor will get his lab and will never see the light of day. He'll be happy as Larry. But Alice you can't say anything about this again. My dad likes to eavesdrop."

Hara glared at the others and they all nodded their heads. They only had to keep it from her father until he had met with the Rosh. Because in the end it was the Rosh who they had to convince.

Her father and Talen rushed back onto the bridge. Gideon sauntered in behind them both. Hara motioned to Alice and the airship swooped past the dreadnaught who sluggishly tried to follow them. The act was very convincing.

Her father gasped in a breath. "The professor is dead."

Hara nodded. "Do you still want to go to Moscow?"

Her father blinked shocked by her coldness. She didn't wait for his question about her mood. "A prison teaches you to be cold. Do you want to go to Moscow?" She asked again.

Her father nodded thoughtfully. "We still have the vials. Maybe that will be enough."

It probably would be enough for the Rosh as their aim was to cripple the Empire. They didn't need the professor for that.

Hara wasn't surprised to see Gideon lounging on her bed when she went to her room that night.

She asked, "The case?"

"Sorted," Gideon said casually.

Hara frowned and he added, "They won't know it isn't the real stuff. Trust me."

She shook her head. "This is my father's plan. His plans always fall to pieces and I'm usually the one holding the bag at the end of it."

Gideon patted the bed next to him and she sat down. He tucked her in against him and she let him. They were quiet for a long moment.

Hara said, "The last time my dad was around, he planned to con people out of a lot of money. He had me build a digging tool and told them it would cut

171

down on costs to mine and he had a mine in Africa. It was all going to plan when one man went to Africa and came back and he knew about the fake mines. He attacked my father. Dad almost killed him. He ran for it, but I had been knocked unconscious in the fight and I was arrested."

Gideon didn't say anything but his arm around her tightened. She continued, "When I woke up they had arrested me. They discovered I was a woman so they took me to the judge who was trying my case. He listened to my story."

Hara sighed at the memories. If the judge hadn't taken pity on her, she would be dead. Prison was no laughing matter. Instead, he had given her community service to pay for her crimes.

Gideon ran a hand over her hair. She accepted comfort. "My dad didn't even check on me. He didn't care if I was alive or dead. I realised then he wasn't my father. But I was still so angry."

Gideon's voice showed his understanding. "So this is for you."

Hara nodded. "I need to cut ties with my father in a way that it is my choice. This is a farewell."

Gideon said, "When we release something from our collection there is a ritual which we do." She smiled glad he understood.

He asked, "Are you going to be part of my collection?"

Hara rested her head on his shoulder. "Let me finish with my father and then I'll give you an answer."

Gideon didn't push and that made her want to give in.

Hara flipped the switch and turned off the air pump. She had been putting in something to help the boys shovel in the coal.

Liam asked, "Is that it?"

She grinned at him. "I know it seems simple, but that joint there which holds that arm took me almost two years to perfect. Everything in here is a culmination of thousands of clever people putting together the bits they are good at. Now help me pack up these tools. A Tinker always looks after their tools."

Liam was an eager lad and he was good at the work as well, though she doubted he would be as imaginative as her Opa when it came to making something new.

There was a screech. Like the sound of metal on metal. Liam lifted his head and he was about to go see what it was but she waved him back to packing up. She heard the sound again and followed it to the back of the engine room.

Hara also heard Marvin curse. "Ouch! You cursed little creature. Stop wriggling. I just need to get to your off switch and when you wake up again, you will be in the lap of luxury."

Anger burned through Hara. She grabbed the shovel which was hanging up. She didn't announce herself, she just stepped around the corner and swung the shovel.

She caught her father on the back of his head. He collapsed in an unceremonious lump.

Angel twittered and struggled to get out of Marvin's grip. She dumped the shovel and crouched to free Angel. Hara muttered a curse at her father.

Angel clicked her metal teeth in agreement and scrambled up Hara's arm the moment she was free. Angel turned on her shoulder to hiss at Marvin's prone form.

Hara stood up and picked up the shovel to put it away. After all, a tinker looks after their tools.

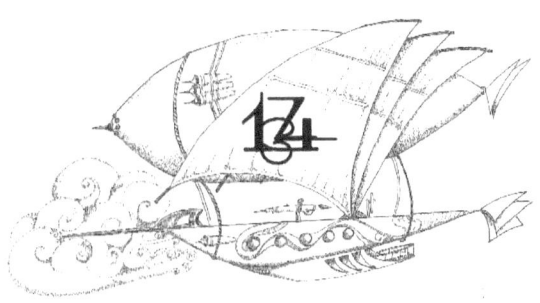

Gideon found Marvin on the deck drinking. He smiled at Gideon when he approached and motioned for him to share a drink. Gideon approach, but he didn't take the flask.

Gideon tucked his hands in his pockets to make sure he didn't do anything stupid. "Do you care about your daughter?"

"Hara? Of course. She is a brilliant engineer. It runs in the family," he said nonchalantly.

From what Hara had told him, Marvin couldn't put a travelling set together. Gideon studied him for a long moment, then asked, "What do you want from Hara?"

Marvin snorted. "Want? We are family. There isn't an account of checks and balances between us."

Gideon startled Marvin by grabbing him by his shirt and lifting him until Marvin was on his toes. Marvin squeaked but Gideon's hold made it hard to make a loud noise. Gideon's voice when he spoke was deadpanned. "You are to do nothing to harm Hara. Do you understand me?"

The jovial light went from Marvin's eyes. "You forget yourself lizard. Hara is my daughter and she will come back to me over and over because she is family. There is nothing you can do about the blood we share."

Gideon dropped him. "Just stay away from her. Your blood is weak Marvin and Hara is strong. She will be in my collection and she will turn from you."

Marvin snorted. "You are dreaming lizard. She always comes back crawling." Gideon shook his head at the delusions of the man.

Hara checked on the gauges of the hydraulics. She had been tweaking the system and wanted to be sure she wasn't putting undue pressure on it all.

She heard Gideon say in a sing song voice. "If I take these two away how many would I have left?"

For a moment she wondered if Gideon was having lessons with Liam but the maths seemed too simple for the clever boy. Curious Hara made sure she was quiet as she peered around the corner.

Gideon was sitting on the floor cross legged with coffee beans in front of him. He was shifting beans from one pile to the other. Angel sat in front of him and shifted her small claws to indicate a number.

Gideon beamed and said excitedly, "Yes! Yes, that is right. Okay, let's try another one."

Hara pressed her back against the wall and covered her mouth. The urge to laugh was extreme. So much for Gideon hating Angel. Angel was clever but like an animal clever. To teach her to count would have taken hours.

Once Hara had her urge to laugh under control she left as quietly as she had arrived. This was one little secret she would keep to herself until she needed a good reason to tease Gideon. Knowing him it wouldn't be very long.

<hr>

Hara woke up from a doze and realised she had fallen asleep against Gideon. They had been taking turns looking after the supposed vials. She blinked her sleep addled eyes. She realised she had woken because there was someone outside the door. It opened without a knock and the other dragon came in.

She said, "You could have knocked."

The dragon looked at Gideon first before he turned to her. "I do not want anyone to know I am here. Did the ruse work?"

Hara nodded. "My father is going to take the vials to the Rosh."

Harlen seemed to be hesitating about something, but he must have come to a decision as he said, "It would please the Empire if this ship were no longer a privateer. To that end, I offer some information. The member of parliament you deal with has some of her dirty fingers in diamonds her fellow Roshians are unaware of."

Hara raised an eyebrow. This was the kind of information which could free her and their ship. Gideon said, "I will dispose of the poison in our old world."

Harlen raised an eyebrow. "Is that wise?"

Gideon said, "It only works on the bonded."

Harlen looked thoughtful and she wondered if he was going to ask for the poison, but in the end he shook his head. "Later."

He left them without another word. Hara twisted her head so she could look at Gideon. "What are you doing in my bed by the way?"

All she remembered was talking to him earlier in the evening and being tired. He should have returned to his own room. They didn't need two people watching the vials. He answered without any hesitation. "Having my arm go to sleep."

She punched him in the arm and when he glared at her she asked, "Better?"

She asked after a long silence, "Why would the poison work on bonded dragons and not others?"

He was quiet for long enough that she wondered if he would answer at all.

Eventually he said, "To explain it I would have to tell you more about my people."

He was quiet for a moment but she didn't push him. He would answer her when he was ready. "If you took a rock and crushed it what would you get?"

"Pebbles probably. Sand if you really crushed it small."

"People are like that. We are all made up of things that seem solid but are made up of really tiny things. These tiny things act very strange. They don't always stay inside you. Sometimes they go to the in-between and sometimes they even travel all the way to my former home. When we travelled the in-between we wanted to look like something that lived in your world. It helped us to travel that distance as well as the in-between is not kind to things which are alive."

"Like flowers?"

His voice showed he was smiling. "Yes, like flowers. When we travelled the in between to come to this world we borrowed the small tiny things that make up a person but only the bits that were in the in-between. When they returned to this world they remembered their shape and what they were and this allows us to be shaped like a human."

Curious she asked, "Could you pick what you looked like?"

"Yes, in a way. We didn't know whether the shapes we picked would be pleasing to your people. Instead we picked forms which would be useful."

His fingers stroked through her hair. "Is this form pleasing to you?"

She snorted. "Get back to the story Gideon."

"All of us which came over to this world are made up of bits of this world but mostly we are made up of tiny small stuff that comes from our home world. That means things in this world can affect only a small part of us as the small tiny bits from our home world doesn't work the same way as the small tiny bits from your world."

"What about the dragons who are bonded to people here?"

"Most of them are men as most of our women stayed in our home plane. We discovered that we can make our small tiny bits tangle up with a person's small tiny bits."

She chuckled. "I know the birds and the bees, Gideon, you don't have to explain how sex works."

She could feel his own chuckle as she was still lying on his chest. She really should yell at him for sneaking into her room but he was a dragon and she knew it would be wasted breath.

"By making our small tiny stuff tangle up with your small tiny wee bits means that our small bits act the

179

same way and that means we can be affected by things in this world more. We are still different from humans but when we are bonded, more of ourselves are here and not like what we were in our home world."

He was quiet for a long while so Hara felt comfortable to ask, "Do you really want to bond with me?"

He let out a soft breath. "More than anything in two worlds."

***

Hara shrugged on her fur coat and tucked her hands into the pockets. Angel was again curled in the fold of her collar. It was warmer here than the inhospitable area the Professor had his cabin but the cold of Moscow could still make Angel a bit sluggish.

Hara stepped onto the lift which would take them to the ground. Slower it was also safer because of the vials. Gideon carried the case of vials. He carefully guarded it as if he still believed the poison was inside.

Marvin said, "Come along, we are meeting Marya in a warehouse."

Gideon and Hara exchanged looks. It didn't sit well with her that her father's contact was Marya.

Marvin asked, "Are all the vials there?"

Gideon answered, "Every last one."

It looked like her father was going to say something, but he just wrinkled his face and shook his head. They left the Blazing Blunderbuss.

Hara was nervous on many levels. Would they be able to fool Marya? Would they be able to convince Marya to leave them alone? This would be their only chance to get free without dirtying their hands first.

She looked at Gideon, and he didn't seem worried in the least. She took some strength from that. The warehouse where they had met Marya before was the same one they were using this time. Gideon raised an eyebrow at Hara and she returned it.

Her father seemed oblivious. He strolled into the warehouse and called out, "Marya, sweetheart."

Hara rolled her eyes. Her father had never cared for anyone but himself. Though he did have a track record of wining and dining many women. Usually for one of his cons. Marya though, wasn't one to fall for shallow endearments and charms.

When she came out of the shadows she threw her arms around Marvin and he spun her around.

Hara sighed. "You two can quit the act. You two are sharks."

Marya blinked at her. "I didn't expect you."

Hara was tired of the lies. "Yes you did. You wouldn't have met us if you weren't aware of everything."

Marya's eyes sparked. Marvin said, "What is this, my dear? Are you known to my lovely daughter?"

Marya stepped back. "Fine no acts. Yes, yes, I knew you were on your way and you have completely bungled the operation."

Marvin opened his mouth probably to profess his innocence but Marya waved it off. "Quit it Marvin. You were useful. There is no need to act."

Gideon placed the case down. "This is what you want."

Marya looked at it, but didn't move towards the case. She turned to Marvin. "Tell me what happened to the doctor."

181

Marvin waved his hands dramatically. "We were attacked by the Empire with their massive airship and a dragon came out of nowhere and knocked the doctor off the deck. He splattered on the ground below. He was dead instantly. Man, I heard his scream and how it cut off so suddenly. I must say Marya I'm truly sorry about that. I really did intend to bring him. But we did bring you the vials. There should be enough there to deal with all the trouble you can find."

Marya nodded. "Well, our deal included money for the vials and the doctor and since you only provided half of the deal I think I'll let you leave here alive."

Marvin went red in his face with his own anger. "What? What about my money?"

Hara put her hand on her father's shoulder. "Don't sweat it, dad."

He always wanted to push it. He didn't even notice the gun in Marya's hand. Hara said to Marya, "Now that your business with my father is done, I have something of my own to say. I don't think the pirate life is for me." Then significantly she said, "I'm a bit of a *diamond* in the rough, but I'm not that rough."

Marya shot her a look which could cut. It was clear she got the reference to the diamonds. She clicked the hammer back on the gun, then changed her mind and set it back. Marya's face was stormy. She motioned to someone in the back and a man came to pick up the case.

As the man took away the case Marya said, "Fine you can have your freedom."

Her actions after that were so fast none of them had time to react. Marya pulled the trigger of her gun and spun on her heels and stormed out after the man with a case. Pain flowered in Hara's stomach and her legs became jelly. She stumbled to her knees. Angel came out of her hiding place and trilled entreatingly.

Hara heard people moving, but it was only Gideon, who came to her side. He caught her and eased her onto the ground. He looked serious, but not worried. Angel moved from her collar and climbed his arm to sit on his shoulder to peer down at her.

Hara asked, "My dad?"

"He is gone sweetheart." Gideon's voice was gentle as he spoke.

Hara nodded. Only vaguely surprised she wasn't hurt by her father's desertion. Gideon smoothed her hair away from her face. "Do you trust me, my love?"

She looked at Gideon and nodded her head. He was here when anyone else would have left her.

Gideon said softly, "You are dying. But it doesn't have to be that way. If you are in my collection you can live."

Hara wrinkled her nose and then let out a breath. "Fine."

He would look after her a lot better than her father. His voice was fading away. He patted her face and she focused.

Gideon said firmly, "You need to give me your hands."

Hara lifted one, but the other wasn't working so well. She felt his hand touch both her hands and she closed her eyes. His hands tightened on hers and then warmth threaded through her hands. It got hotter though, and soon was uncomfortable. It escalated to fire just under her skin.

She squirmed and Gideon's hold on her tightened.

He said by her ear, "Almost there, sweetheart almost."

Fire burned through her stomach and she swore she could feel the bullet moving inside her. There was a tinkle of metal on concrete and she opened her eyes. Angel was on the ground and the small metal bullet was in her tiny hands. Holding it against her chest. Hara turned her attention though to her own body. There were black tattoos or brands on her arms.

There was a significant puddle of blood and she closed her eyes again. The pain was gone, but Gideon was still holding onto her. He shifted her so she was half sitting up. She turned her head against his chest and just lay there for a while.

Without opening her eyes, she placed her hand on her stomach. She could feel where the bullet went through her shirt and she felt for the wound underneath. There wasn't even a scar. She opened her eyes when Angel lightly touched her hand with her metal claw. The bullet was nowhere to be seen. Once Hara's eyes were open Angel clicked her tongue and moved so she was again on her shoulder.

There were delicate black tattoos etched into her skin. She could see them on her hand.

Hara said, "I take it there are a few things about this collection thing which you didn't tell me about."

Gideon rumbled a soft, comforting sound. "Yeah, your life force is bound to mine. It means you get to live as long as I do."

She asked, "How long is that?"

He shrugged. "Mmm, we aren't sure. On our own planet we live for a few hundred years, but here we seem to live longer. Especially if we are bound to humans. Our best guess is over a thousand years. Our

Emperor who married a human woman four hundred years ago is already over a thousand."

Gideon rubbed his nose in her hair. "You alright to move? I would kiss you, but it is your turn."

Hara huffed at that confession. She took stock of herself and nodded so he helped her to her feet. She looked around, but there was no sign of her father. She didn't think he would be back at the Blazing Blunderbuss either.

She stopped for a moment and said softly, "Bye dad."

As they left she asked, "You swapped out all of the poison? You didn't miss one of the vials or anything. Because you are now a bonded dragon and you can be in danger."

His voice held a smile as he answered, "Oh, I got all of them. I swapped them the first night."

Hara shook her head. "Never liked poisons. Too sneaky."

Gideon stopped. "That reminds me." He pulled something out of his pocket and left it in the pool of blood she had left.

Hara asked, "What is that?"

"A Diamond. I want to remind Marya."

Clever but she was too tired to even say that.

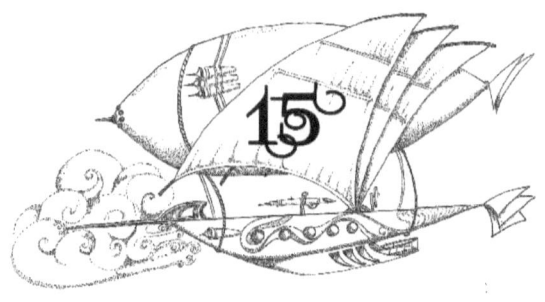

When they returned to the Blazing Blunderbuss Hara wasn't astonished when her father wasn't there.

Alice asked, "Are you alright?"

Liam was standing watch with her and gasped. "That is blood."

Liam went to help her, but Hara waved them off. "I'm fine."

Hara didn't tell them she doubted there was much which could kill her with Gideon nearby.

Talen came out from further in the ship. "There is a message for you."

Hara frowned, wondering if it might be from her father. Talen passed over the note. It had one sentence on it: *You are free.* It was signed Marya.

Talen asked, "Where is Marvin?"

Talen was eying the blood on her clothes and the tattoos, which threaded up her arms so his voice was distracted.

Hara said, "Gone and probably for good."

Especially as he thought she was dead. She wasn't about to correct his misconception. Talen motioned to her blood and the new tattoos. "What happened?"

Hara leaned heavily on Gideon. She was still shaky and besides she liked the way he felt. "I was shot.

Gideon saved me. That is all that matters. Now I think we should leave Moscow. I'm feeling like some sunshine."

She said to Alice, "Get us out of here. I'm going to go change."

Hara pulled her shirt away from her skin. The blood was tacky and it made a sick noise.

Hara winced as she said, "I liked this shirt."

Gideon went to follow her but she waved him off. Now that she realised how terrible the blood really was all she wanted to do was to get clean.

Talen followed. "Hara what is with the tattoos?"

Hara looked at them a little closer and realised they were actually a pattern of geometric designs with a silhouette of a dragon flying.

She twisted her arms. "I think it means I married Gideon."

She smoothed her hands over the tattoos and Talen asked, "And you are alright with that?"

"Mmm probably. But Gideon won't push it."
She smiled as she said that. One thing she was very sure of was that Gideon wouldn't force her to do anything.

Hara stopped and turned to Talen. "Talen I don't need someone to replace dad. He was never really my father. Alfred raised me and he likes Gideon. You need to get over yourself."

Talen pursed his lips. "I don't want to be your dad."

"I know Talen but you are too much like Marvin to be anything else to me but a friend. A close friend, but only a friend."

He nodded and walked away. Gideon said, "Do you think he will back off?"

Hara smiled as she hadn't heard him following them. Though she had assumed he wouldn't be far away.

She shrugged. "Thanks for letting me tell him in my own way."

Gideon shrugged and followed her as she entered her room. She said, "I don't think I'm ready…"

He nodded and caught her arms and tugged her closer. "I know." He leant down and kissed her cheek. "It's still your turn." She smiled and turned her head to kiss him. It was still light and soft, she wasn't ready for anything more. It felt so right. But she really needed to get out of her clothes.

She put her hands on his chest and pushed him back until he was outside her room. She stepped back and closed the door on his face. She chuckled at the look he gave her but he didn't open the door even though she left it unlocked. Dragons had no sense of personal space but it seemed Gideon would give her some.

———◆———

Hara said, "I feel silly. Do I have to do this?" Gideon placed the things needed on a small table. He said, "Trust me it will make you feel better."

She glared at the back of his head as he bent over and rearranged everything on the table. She didn't argue with him anymore because she thought he might be right.

Hara hadn't been able to sleep the night before. She had been worrying about her father. The bastard. Even when he wasn't there he bothered her. Marvin was more than capable of looking after herself and he certainly wasn't part of her crew.

They still hadn't heard anything from him but she doubted she would.

They were still in Moscow. Alice had managed to get them a cargo but it was only being delivered in the morning. Hara would have preferred to have been on their way now that they were free from their obligations to Rosha. Hara didn't trust Marya to stay complacent.

Gideon stepped back from the table. "There."

He motioned her forward and she stepped up to the table. On the table was a small drawing of her father. A bowl, a candle and a small jug.

Gideon gestured to the table. "Take up the picture and say these words."

She picked up the picture and repeated after him as he said, "I give you back to the winds. I give you back to the land."

Gideon motioned to the bowl and she placed the picture inside. He picked up a taper and lit it on the candle and gave it to her. She set it to the picture in the bowl and said without prompting. "I give you back to the fire."

Her voice actually cracked with emotion. Gideon nodded solemnly as they watched the parchment burn. Without prompting she picked up small jug and said in a mere whisper, "This I give you back to the water."

She poured the water into the bowl. It turned grey with the ash and bits of parchment floated to the top. Gideon said in an equally soft voice, "I give my cares and my worries away. I give my love and my duty away. Be free."

She repeated what he said and it really did feel better. She blinked rapidly. When she looked up at Gideon he saw that as a signal and moved to wrap his arms around her. She pressed her face to his chest but the tears caught in her chest making it ache.

Gideon stroked his hand through her hair but didn't say anything more.

Gideon found Marvin in a pleasant hotel in the posh sector in Moscow. He was in the lounge and very drunk. He was waving his cup at a waiter asking for more.

Gideon stopped in front of him. Marvin frowned as at him, until he finally placed him. "Ah the dragon. What brings you here? Are you going to kill me?"

Gideon shook his head and pushed the sleeves up of his shirt. Marvin had been in enough noble circles to know what the tattoos on his arms meant.

Marvin raised an eyebrow. "So you claimed her. I take it she is still alive. Man, I really didn't think Marya had the guts to shoot someone."

Gideon covered his arms again. "That is because you don't see people, you only see what you want to see."

Working on the buttons at his wrist Gideon continued, "You are to leave her alone."

Marvin put his cup down and stood up but he had forgotten how drunk he was and his legs struggled to keep him upright.

He recovered quickly and poked Gideon's chest with a finger. "I told you once she is my girl and in the end she will do anything for me."

Gideon shook his head. "She didn't do this for you. She did this to find a way to be herself. Now she is free, she will never need you in her life. She can move on."

Marvin snorted. "We'll see."

Both of them looked to the side when Talen said, "No, you will leave her alone."

Gideon was astonished. He hadn't sensed the man approaching and Gideon was very good at that.

Talen moved closer. "Hara is not your family any more Marvin. You left her for dead. You don't do that to family. So you go on believing she is dead and stay out of her life. If you don't, then you will have more than the dragon to worry about."

Marvin grunted and sat back down. A servant came up and filled his glass. He gave a cocky grin. "Fine. Have it your way." He waved them off.

Gideon and Talen walked away. After a moment Gideon said, "Thank you."

Talen said coldly, "Just treat her right or you will have to worry about me. You understand?"

Gideon raised an eyebrow. "Really?"

"Really. And you better take me seriously."

"Oh, I do. I didn't hear you sneaking up before. You are one fine sneak. I want to be able to sleep at night."

Talen snorted at Gideon's teasing.

───────◆───────

Hara pointed to something and Liam reached forward to tighten it. The two of them stepped back and Hara said, "Well, turn it on. You aren't going to see if it works unless you test it."

Liam grinned and flipped the switch. The engine turned over and he whooped. Hara grinned at her student. She turned, expecting Gideon to be there and he was.

She smiled at him. "We just doubled our power output thanks to Liam here."

Liam blushed. "It was nothing. Hara showed me how to make the engine more efficient."

Gideon stepped forward and looked over the engine. He asked, "What does it run on?"

Hara grinned. "Water."

He shook his head and said, "This is no steam engine."

She shrugged. Though it ran on water, she wouldn't call it a steam engine either. She motioned to Liam to carry on with his testing and turned to walk out with Gideon. He offered an arm and she took it and leaned in against him.

Hara said, "It means we will be able to get to places quicker. We can take on priority cargo. It should be more lucrative."

They walked out onto the deck. There was no one else there. They came to the railing and she let go of his arm to lean on the railing. Angel came out of her hiding place to take her usual place on the railing. She tilted her head and opened her wings a little. Most likely pretending she was the one flying instead of the Blazing Blunderbuss.

Hara took a deep breath Gideon asked behind her. "Are you happy here?"

She glanced behind her to look at him. She said, "Yeah, I am."

She realised then she had no idea what his feelings were when it came to the Blazing Blunderbuss. She reached out for him and tugged on his shirt so he was closer. "Do you like it here? I can always take you back to your apartment in the city."

Gideon shook his head and stepped even closer. He said, "We are two made one."

Hara wrinkled her nose. "You say that but…"

He nodded. "I know you are not ready for more than what we have now. I have lived for a very long time. I can wait."

She smiled up at him. "I trust you, you know. Not like other men."

She put her arms around his neck. "I think I can handle a few kisses for the moment. We don't have to take turns."

He bowed his head and lightly brushed his lips over hers. He pulled back a little. "I think I can handle a few kisses as well."

He kissed her again but this time he was fierce. Claiming her and she loved it.

About the Author

Nix Whittaker is a high school teacher tucked away in the middle of the North Island of New Zealand. She immigrated to New Zealand when she was a young girl from South Africa and has completely embraced the New Zealand life.

She has been writing from a young age when she read all the books available for people her age and was forced to write her own just to feed her voracious appetite for Literature.

She studied at Auckland University, but opted for a quiet life in teaching. Where she can help her fellow neurodivergents find a place where they belong. She lives with her cats and writes between planning lessons and socialising with friends.

You can contact her at Reshwity@gmail.com
Or follow her on Facebook or Tiktok.
Or her website www.nixwhittaker.com

Thank You

I have enjoyed writing this book and I hope you enjoyed reading it as well.

Please write a review for this book. Your voice is important.

Sincerely,

Nix Whittaker